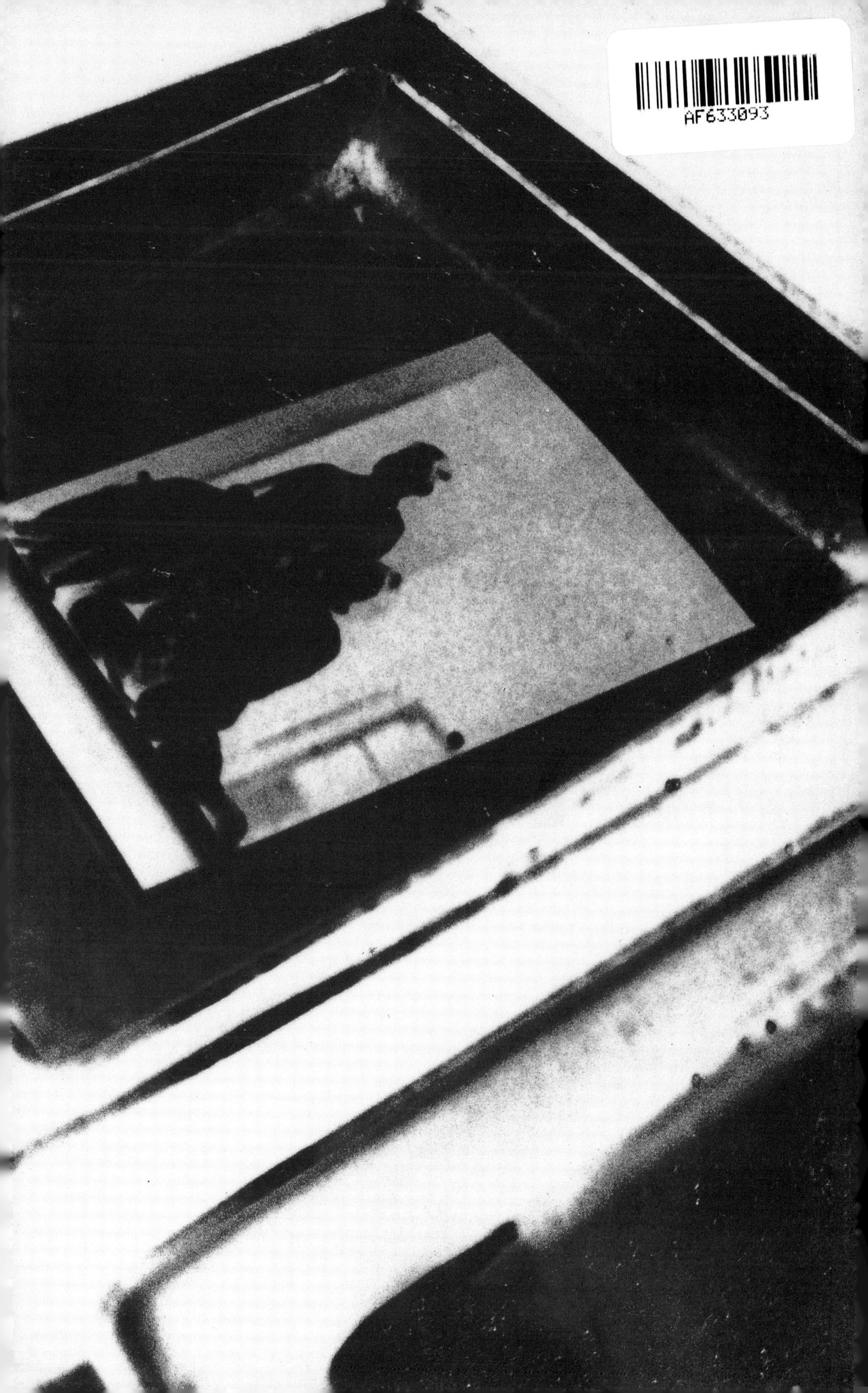

Dramatic Moments

Photographs and Memories of Calcutta Theatre from the Sixties to the Nineties

Dramatic Moments

Photographs and Memories of Calcutta Theatre from the Sixties to the Nineties

Nemai Ghosh

Seagull
BOOKS
CALCUTTA 2000

Designed by Naveen Kishore
Cover and endpaper photographs by Nemai Ghosh
ISBN 81 7046 156 1

Published by Naveen Kishore
Seagull Books Private Limited,
26 Circus Avenue, Calcutta 700 017
Processed by Jasra Graphics Private Limited,
Unit One, First Floor, Prabhadevi Industrial Estate,
408, Veer Savarkar Marg, Prabhadevi, Mumbai 400 025
Printed in India by Pragati Art Printers,
17, Red Hills, Hyderabad 500 004

Contents

Preface

I cannot clearly recall at this point of time what attracted me so greatly to theatre. In all probability, it was my desire to find some meaning in what I did or wished to do that drew me closer to those bright spotlights, which shine on the stage and illuminate and immortalize so many men, moments and memories. It was not a journey for a place in the sun but for a small footprint on the path treaded by so many legends of the Bengali theatre. Yes, theatre was and is truly my first love. It had seeped into my system much before I realized that it had. Soon it translated into a phase of eventful changes. From the makeshift stages of college plays, it moved on to a committed, mature and serious platform of Utpal Dutt's Little Theatre Group, which became the nurturing ground of my passion and respect for the art. In a short time the distance between the people I had admired from a seat in the audience and me was gone. I became part of one big family and developed a strong sense of belonging with it. It was a bond that was not to be weakened by time. But as fate would have it, my exploits on the stage did not last for very long. One fine day, an unexpected gift and a gifted man changed everything. The gift was a camera and the gifted man—Satyajit Ray. The sheer charisma of that man drew me away from what I claim was my first love. All that I was left with was a camera in my hand and an obsession to follow that gifted man. But at no point of time did I lose my touch with theatre and its progress. Maybe I was no longer a part of it, but I watched from a distance through the lenses of my camera. It was as if the camera was an extension of myself that built an invisible bridge between me and the stage.

As a photographer, the most fascinating aspect that attracted me towards theatre was the light on the stage. It was, indeed, a very challenging proposition. As I grew more confident after the first few plays that I shot, *Pagla Ghora* (Bohurupee) and *Manusher Adhikarey* (Little Theatre Group), my desire to continue gained momentum. My inspiration came from individuals like Tapas Sen, the renowned lighting designer, Shombhu Banerjee (photographer) and B.K. Sanyal (mejda). I witnessed and photographed some of the legendary productions of Bengali theatre and recorded the growth of the group theatre movement. Through the years I have missed out on very little that has happened in this art form. In retrospect, all seems to be an experience of a lifetime. When I look at the images of that bygone era it evokes feelings of pride and nostalgia, and also a sense of loss. I have always wished that there should be some kind of a visual record of that period of Bengali theatre which would enrich the sensibilities of the future generations of actors, directors and producers: the inheritors of a wonderful legacy.

Having said that, I would like to stress that this volume is a very personal journey down memory lane, with no attempt at claiming either an all-encompassing or objective documentation of theatre history. Needless to say, selecting from my vast store of photographs has been a difficult exercise—including all the productions I have shot has simply not been possible.

This album, a long cherished dream of mine, has finally come about. In this context, I should specially like to thank the publishers who have given a form to my vision and Samik Bandyopadhyay for his text. I also wish to thank Bikash Bose and my son Satyaki for their meaningful support. I am also much indebted to my wife Shibani, my eldest son Santanu and daughter Sharmistha, as well as to all the other members of my joint family, especially my brothers Netai, Chittoranjan, Swadeshranjan, and Nisithranjan, for supporting and encouraging me in my creative field. Last but not the least, I thank all the members of the theatre fraternity without whom this project would never have seen the light of day.

Nemai Ghosh

Sombhu Mitra

Sombhu Mitra (1915-97), in his theatrical career, represented a seamless continuity between the histrionics of the century-old Bengali actor–managerial tradition and the New Bengali Theatre that began with *Nabanna* ('The New Harvest,' 1944), which he directed, along with the playwright, Bijan Bhattacharya (1915-78), for the Indian People's Theatre Association (IPTA), a 'front' organization of the Communist Party. But for the rest of his career, he went on distancing himself farther and farther from political commitment, and eventually from theatre itself, spending the last twenty-five years of his life in virtual retirement. Already, in 1948, when he left the IPTA to form his own group, Bohurupee (which still remains active), he had spelt out his credo quite simply as 'producing good plays well.'

Bohurupee consisted of a group of committed actresses, actors and technicians, almost all of them formally untrained and self-taught, and professionally engaged outside theatre, held together by a missionary zeal for the 'honest theatre' and their unquestioning loyalty to the director. Without a theatre of its own, Bohurupee would perform at one night stands in several regular theatres or makeshift spaces in Calcutta and the small district towns of the state of West Bengal, occasionally touring other metropolitan centres of the country. It became the model for several such groups that emerged in Calcutta and elsewhere in later years. Most of the theatre works documented in the following pages, are products of this particular mode of theatre practice—a theatre that is non-professional in a literal sense, but with a professional discipline and code of values that often strike a fairly high level of creativity, drawing on a substantial dose of idealistic motivation.

In an initial urge to break free from the melodramatic conventions of late nineteenth and early twentieth century Bengali theatre (drawing on late nineteenth century British melodrama), Mitra, in his earliest phase, fell back on nineteenth-century European realism, producing adaptations of Ibsen's *An Enemy of the People* [*Dashachakra* ('The trap that the mob weaves'), 1952] and *A Doll's House* [*Putulkhela* ('Playing with a doll'), 1958]; setting a pattern of indigenization that too often used the narrative framework and dramatic structure of the original to frame a politics or an attitude quite different from that in the original.

In the two Ibsen plays and his dramatization of Rabindranath Tagore's *Char Adhyay* ['Four Chapters.' Originally published in 1934, translation in English published in 1950; dramatization by Mitra, produced by Bohurupee, 1951], Mitra assumed a liberal, humanist position as he addressed some of the issues that he felt needed to be redefined in a postcolonial, newly independent society, e.g. those of the complex dynamics involving the manipulation of public opinion in a democracy, the mobilization of violence against the State by an organized underground political force, and man-woman relations in the family space. In his staging, particularly in the scenography designed by Khaled Chowdhury and illuminated by Tapas Sen, and in the elaborately modulated articulation of the text, Mitra was already moving away from the realistic, reaching out to an 'extra-realistic' style of expression beyond the realistic representation of characters.

It was through *Char Adhyay* that Mitra re-discovered Tagore, who offered him a different dramaturgy, rooted in mythicization of the immediate reality, and a rich poetry that called for continuous interpretation/unravelling in theatric terms, and a different 'quest' altogether—for the 'core of the social sensibility, where the peasants, the workers, the zamindars and jotedars cannot be differentiated any longer, where there lies a morality at the centre of a society that encompasses them all. There are people who insist that the only job for the progressive artist is to take his position on the side of the peasants against the zamindars and jotedars, on the side of the workers against their employers, and arouse a hatred strong enough to ignite a civil war with the revolutionary potential of building up to a revolution that would bring the social order toppling down. For them, it would be a reactionary venture to seek the core of the society's sensibility when the time is ripe to create a new art, a new culture, which has to be a proletarian art, a proletarian culture.'

With *Raktakarabi* [written originally in 1924, translated as *Red Oleanders* in 1925, produced by Bohurupee in 1954], Mitra 'realized that *Raktakarabi* was a distinctive form of Indian theatrical expression. For example, it uses multiple actions within a single dramatic area and presents inner and outer life, and the individual and the symbol simultaneously.' The quest for an 'Indian' theatre continued till the other Tagore play *Raja* [written originally in 1910, translated as *King of the Dark Chamber* in 1914, produced by Bohurupee in 1964]—seeking to achieve, through a minimal use of sets and furniture, a space that could place the characters 'clearly against the sky,' and offer the audience the spell of a quieter theatricality very different from 'dramatic conflict in the European manner.' For a while, Mitra played with a vision of a poetic theatre, building from Tagore, exploring the possibility of weaving images out of the utterance of words, letting sounds, tones, rhythm and pace shape/define the meaning; and the use of the body in a manner that would make 'the actor's movements, turns, and stands full of beauty and poetry, and yet the style that would convey this suggestion would avoid exaggeration, and stay close enough to the real, skirting the real, the way poetry flows close to the idiom of its own time, touching its edges all the time.'

Mitra never repudiated his 'vision' of the 'Indian' theatre, but in his last few productions, that included Badal Sircar's *Baki Itihas* (1967) and *Pagla Ghora* (1971) and Tendulkar's *Shantata! Court Chalu Ahe* (1971), Mitra had returned to the realistic mode, with theatre almost totally confined to *speaking*, with shades and variations of moods and tones. In 1971, Mitra directed a play for the last time; in 1978 he left Bohurupee. For the last twenty years of his life, he remained a proud, lonely man, making occasional appearaces in productions like Brecht's *Galileo*, in Bengali, directed by Fritz Bennewitz, for a limited number of performances. The photographs illustrate two other such productions directed by other directors,

Mudrarakshasa, directed by Ajitesh Bandyopadhyay, and *Tughlaq*, directed by Shyamanand Jalan. In these performances, Mitra stood out from the rest in a distinctive style of articulation, and with a presence that was magnetic; the production, often losing its balance in the process, left the audience wondering at Mitra's mastery over voice and stance.

The short-lived quest for an 'Indian theatre' and his experiments with Tagore notwithstanding, Mitra remained a thorough Stanislavskian, centring on the characters, finding a foolproof psychological rationale for their actions, and providing a manner of speaking and an idiom of gestures to underscore it—'explaining' the character away—backing it up with the necessary details of a physical setting; and directing the lighting to illuminate the character in his changing moods and in his space. As actor, Mitra wielded a well honed voice, moving at ease over several scales, with the skill of controlling his voice and tones to shift and change, to bring out the meaning and charge of particular words and phrases. At times this power of the voice became Mitra's fatal Cleopatra—and once his early designers and fellow actors and actresses left him, his theatre suffered. He had to bear the burden of the performance, responding to the challenge with bravura performance, and little else.

Char Adhyay

Char Adhyay

Char Adhyay

Char Adhyay

Char Adhyay

'The light has gone dim, come closer to me, come closer. My eyes are reaching out to you, praying for a release. You alone can give me that release. It is such a small span. . .' If the passion of love that we experience deep in ourselves had a language of its own, it would be this language: the language which we cannot speak and yet which is the language of our deepest passions—the language of poetry. Acting should attune itself to express naturally the poetry of passion. It cannot be accomplished through a naturalistic style alone. We must find a way to pass easily from the naturalistic plane to the subjective. Exterior and interior life should rub shoulders with each other and remain organically related, in the way in which it was once so natural for Hamlet to move into a soliloquy. Through Tagore, we must find a way to express the whole of a man. We need a voice, a gesture, which would be able to express authentically our most intimate feelings.

Sombhu Mitra

All the components of a stage design are static, while all the other components of a dramatic performance are dynamic. Hence one has to try to give all the objects and forms on stage shapes that would relate to the pattern of movements followed by the performers in a way that would create an impression of dynamism. That is how the performers and the stage design can be animated simultaneously. The director, the stage designer and the lighting designer have to work concertedly to make the stage design an organic part of the production. This was the objective consciously pursued in the Bohurupee *Putulkhela*, which had no walls, for the play did not call for any wall. There were doors and windows, because they were essential. While one of the doors had an arch on top, there was another without an arch, in violation of the rules of architecture. In the first scene, a burst of yellow spread on the doors of the room, the windows, the seats, the bed, had a bewildering impact. The dazzling white, transparent autumn sky seen through the window, heightened by the black blackground, emphasized the intensity of the colour to the point where the exaggeratedly decorated setting laid out by Bulu-Nora swamps her own outline entirely. Then Tapan-Torvald enters from a room, almost totally dark, dressed in dazzling white, with a bright red diary in his hand. He moves to a row of furniture, beginning at extreme left with a small rack with a lampshade on top of it, then raised gradually along a rising curve to the top of the easy chair, and the top of the chair, a clothes stand, a flower vase, a bundle and a cane bowl on the top of a cupboard, culminating with the arch above the door, set with a Ganesha image within the arch; a downward curve beginning with a hat rack, an arched lampshade above a bookrack, a pillow on the bed, the curve ending its falling cycle at a rounded cane stool — creating the image of a human figure crushed by despair, and then looking out in yearning beyond the door opening out to the world outside. These curves constitute the main rhythmic line of the composition of the stage design of *Putulkhela*. And yet they were arranged in such a man-

Putulkhela

ner that the lighting, delicately handled, illuminated at certain points only the straight lines, and at other times only the bow-curve lines. In the second Act, the yellow gives way to a deep blue, and red designs on an ashen surface, making for a grim atmosphere, the premonition of something terrible. At the end of the third Act the same lines draw our mind towards the door opening to the outside world. At the end of it all, a defeated Tapan, bent over the arm of the chair, merges with the pattern of the lines in a declining curve, revealing once and for all the significance of the rhythmic scheme of the stage design.

Khaled Chowdhury

Putulkhela

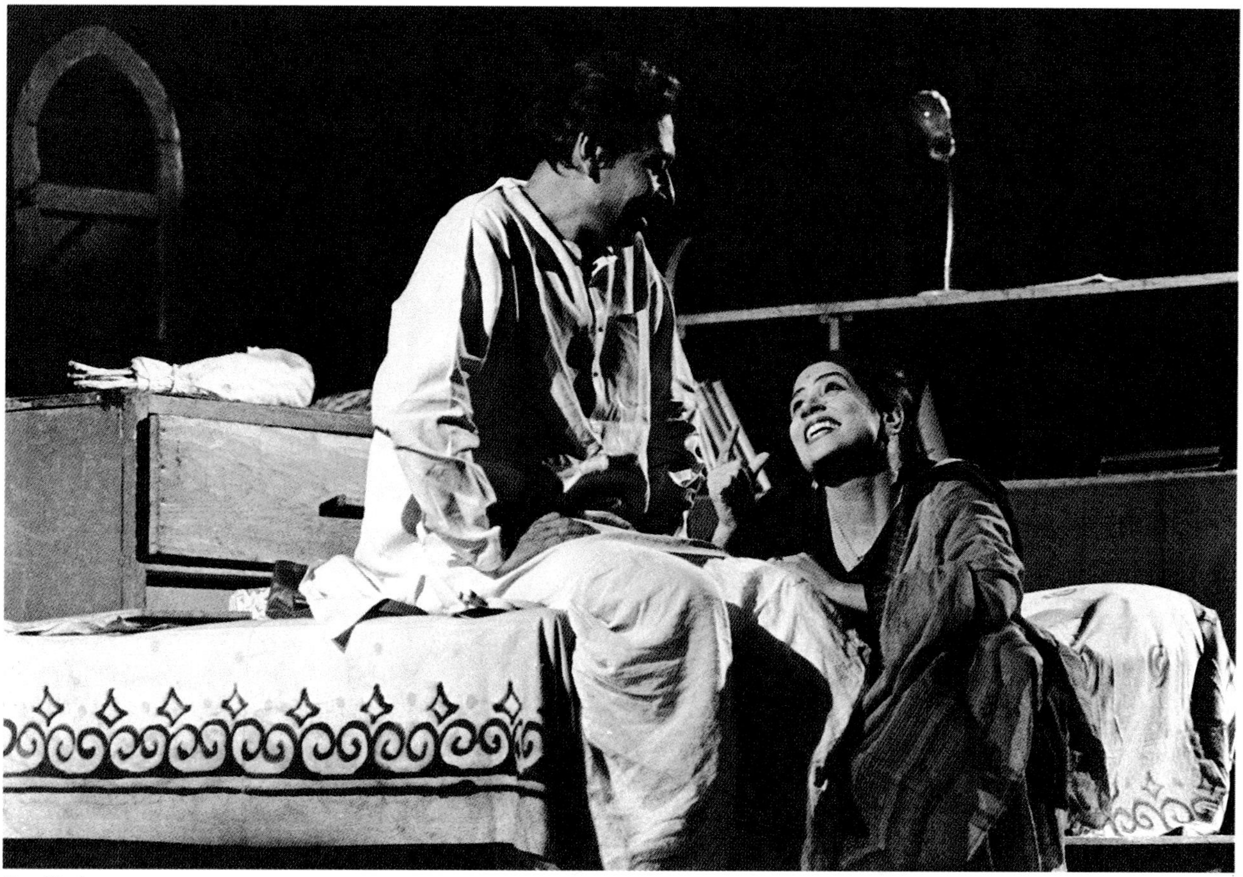

Putulkhela

Putulkhela

Putulkhela

Dashachakra

Enemy of the People (renamed *Dashachakra*) was suggested by the poet Bishnu Dey, who asked Santi Bose, who was a lecturer in some college at the time, to adapt it to the Indian situation. The fundamental point that was there in the original play came out very strongly, since we could relate it to our knowledge of the martyrs who had given their lives for the freedom of the country. That was one of the reasons why we did it. There was another reason. It lay in the feeling that if we are not careful enough, a democracy can land you anywhere. That is what has happened now, when all sorts of things are being done in the name of democracy. The play was a warning to ourselves that we should be careful and not get to play the numbers

Dashachakra

game. To serve the whole of society or humanity at large with what is most important for it, sometimes it is the individual alone who identifies the truth. Think of Darwin—that single man changed the idea of evolution. Think of Marx, whose reading of history has changed the outlook of so many historians after him. Think of Freud, whose ideas have given a new shape to human thoughts. They are all individual human beings, but born out of society. They were living in the society—not saying or discovering these things from outside the society, but from being there, very much inside the society. That's what brought us to this play.

We felt that in the progress of human society, some-

Tughlaq

times, or maybe most of the time, truth comes through an individual. What happens in our civilization is that it's always the statistical man we are talking about. But an individual human being can be very important—an individual who is related to the society—the kind of individual that is necessary for our prosperity through change—a change that can be achieved only through a balance.

Sombhu Mitra

Tughlaq

As I set out to explore the productional possibilities inherent in the Sanskrit plays, I drew inspiration from both V. Shantaram's *Stree*, based on *Abhijnana Shakuntalam*, and Sir Laurence Olivier's version of Shakespeare's *Henry V*. I wondered how I could recreate the age and its environment, discover the productional qualities of the tradition, and make the ultimate experience dynamic and sleek enough for an audience used for ages to a theatre based on European models. An article by Satyajit Ray—'Calm Without: Fire Within'—offered some valuable insights . . .

When I chose *Mudrarakshasa* for my first production of

a Sanskrit play—in a Bengali version—I had Sombhu Mitra as Chanakya. For myself I chose the insignificant role of Chandragupta, which I could easily carry after bearing the productional responsibilities. The fact that the play had little need for actresses was also an advantage. *Mudrarakshasa* is India's oldest political play. Here, for the first time, the common people came to the fore in the theatre. We used a saffron backdrop, with the wings draped with pieces of the *namabali* [piece of cloth, often used as a scarf, bearing inscriptions of the names of divinities], with dangling streamers. To set off Rakshasa's house in Act IV, a red net curtain covered the entire stage. We used a drop curtain or *yavanika*.

To relate the old Sanskrit play to the Bengali sensibility, we made use of the spirit of reverence rooted in the Vedic-Brahmanic associations and the long tradition of *puja* rituals with which the Bengali individual grows up.

Before the curtain rose, the characters entered the Kalamandir auditorium through all the entrances, beating drums and cymbals, carrying sticks and bowls of fragrant incense, and then worshipped the *dhvajadanda*, the sacred pole that marked the site of a traditional performance. The Brahman Chanakya blessed the King. The King offered his compliments to the merchant. The Shudra offered his back to bear the King's shoes. There were 64 actors participating in this scene . . . At the end of the elaborate ritual, Chanakya's first off voice piece removes the action to a different style altogether, closer to modern acting conventions.

Ajitesh Bandyopadhyay

Mudrarakshasa

Galileor Jiban

Pagla Ghora

Chop! Adalat Cholchhey

Raja

Acting as Nora in *A Doll's House,* in Bengali, when I spoke my last speech in the play towards the close, and rubbed the streak of *sindur* off the parting of my hair (instead of taking the marriage ring off, as in the original), I could hear a stifled exclamation rising from the tense silence that held the audience in thrall. That was the point where I felt a thrill at having been able to strike at the minds of the people. As Sudarshana in Tagore's *Raja* (The King of the Dark Chamber), I had to play a role altogether different, a fight with oneself. Who is the King that one never sees? Is it God? But Tagore never describes him as God. In a letter he tells us, 'The human soul has its inner drama.' 'In the play, Sudarshana insisted on having a look at the King who is not to be seen, till she falls for the external charms of the phony King and offers him her garland, only to realize her error and to move to the true union through the shame and suffering of the guilt. One reaches creation through an apocalypse. The Upanishads tell us how the Great Creator glowed with heat, to create. Whatever our soul creates, it creates in incessant pain. But there is something beyond the pain in the pain itself. Beauty lies in the pain; there is happiness in the pain.'

Sudarshana had disrupted the balance when she sought the King within her, outside. When she ultimately discovers her King in the dark chamber of her heart, she transcends herself. An actress acting the role has to come to the core of that final discovery and transcend herself—a difficult task for an actress, an ordinary mortal! How can she raise herself to that space of discovery, of self-realization? But even as I prepared, and through every evening of acting, I was lifted to a space that held the King who was not to be seen and maybe I could lift my audience along with me to that space, too. I felt impatient with all the trappings of the stage itself and sought to break through the space of the stage to a quest through the open space that led to the King. I found it easier to act Jocaste in Sophocles's *Oedipus*, with her fleshy anguish, her sense of sin leading to suicide. The text was rich but easy. I could play at ease with those tones, those expressions. It was easier to thrill the spectators.

Tripti Mitra

Raja

Tripti Mitra

Picked up and forced by her cousin, Bijan Bhattacharya, playwright, director and actor, to step in for a missing actress, in *Aagun* in 1943, Tripti Mitra (1925-89) stayed on in theatre till her death. If she hadn't, she would have preferred to be a physician or a nurse.

Coming into her own as an actress in *Nabanna* (1944), she recalled, late in life, memories of the 1943 Famine that had gone into the making of her role in the play, the role of Binodini, a woman driven by the famine to join the hordes of the rural poor marching to the city of Calcutta to seek sustenance. She recalled, in particular, two moving experiences. One afternoon, serving food in the gruel kitchen to a host of the famine stricken, a peasant wife waiting in the queue died right in her arms; arms that she had stretched out instinctively at the sight of death in the woman's very look. Then there was the starving woman she saw on the street, collecting, from a dripping drainpipe, the water drained out of the boiled rice cooking in someone's upper floor kitchen, shoving her little children away brutally to devour the liquid, before realizing what she had done, and calling her children up to her, holding them, dumb with shock, close to her and offering them consolation!

With deadly honesty and naivete, she would tell her interviewers that in her negotiation with the horror of the famine she acquired her first lessons in acting. As she said later, 'I acted the role of a peasant wife flung upon the streets of Calcutta by hunger, a woman lost in a city of speeding cars, well dressed ladies and gentlemen, foodstuffs piled in shops; a woman in rags begging in a city where the rich, the poor and the middle classes had joined in a mad grab for dirty money. Maybe it was the experience of working among them that gave me the capacity to live the character created by the playwright. I was recognized at once as an actress, but there was greater satisfaction in the fact that my acting brought in more money for the relief fund.'

All her life Tripti Mitra acknowledged with gratitude the rigorous discipline and training that she received from director Sombhu Mitra, whom she married in 1945. In her Bohurupee days she covered a wide range of roles, the best remembered being Phuljan in *Chhenra Taar* (1950 and 1965), Ela in *Char Adhyay* (1951), Nandini in *Raktakarabi* (1954), Bulu in *Putulkhela* (1958), Tarala in *Kanchanranga* (1961), Aparna and Gunabati in *Bisarjan* (1961-62), Jocaste in *Raja Oidipous* (1964), Sudarshana in *Raja* (1964), Basanti and Kana in *Baki Itihas* (1967), and Benare Bai in *Chope! Adalat Cholchhey* (1971): all directed by Sombhu Mitra.

Rooting herself firmly in the real, capturing the most delicate and fleeting details of the character in her setting, she could take those flights that revealed the forces within struggling for expression. In a tribute, Habib Tanvir recalled his first view of Tripti in *Chhenra Taar,* 'as a fumbling village girl, tripping, unable to walk in the new shoes she had obtained in the city, giggling, trying to cover up her embarrassment.'

In *Char Adhyay* and *Putulkhela*, both centring on a man-woman relationship, disintegrating and collapsing, the former in the setting of underground militancy, the latter in that of middle-class domesticity, she played a whole trajectory from the lighthearted flightiness of the openings through gathering shadows to the irredeemable end, registering the process step by step, blow by blow, with never a jerk or a shock, an achievement in the best tradition of strict naturalist regimen. In *Baki Itihas,* Badal Sircar's play about an enlightened literary couple spending a Sunday speculating about and reconstructing the story of a suicide, reported in the morning papers—they have a vague recollection of having met the man once—in parallel dramatic versions, Tripti Mitra played three roles, underlining the *difference* in every appearance with a change of clothes, a little make-up, and details of gait, gesture, look, and tone, adding up to an authentic type, located unmistakably in her social station; as the suicide's wife, in the two different versions, and as the Sunday playwright, she inhabited radically different social spaces, that she practically brought into being, with minimal support from the scenography.

In 1957, she directed Tagore's *Dakghar* ('The Post Office') for Bohurupee, her first directorial venture. She directed her second production thirteen years later—*Kimbadanti* ('Legend'), a play by fellow actor, Kumar Roy. In 1971, playing Benare, a woman trapped by her fellow actors, in *Chope! Adalat Cholchhey,* the Bohurupee version of Vijay Tendulkar's *Shantata! Court Chalu Ahe,* and passing through a series of hurts and humiliations in her personal life, she commissioned *Aparajita*, a one woman play, in which she directed herself, playing eighteen roles, premiering on 7 September 1971. The same year, Richard Schechner, visiting Calcutta, saw 'the last twenty minutes' of *Aparajita*—after 'being bored or worse by the plays I was taken to in Calcutta (mostly in Hindi, mostly directed and performed by well-meaning but inept amateurs),' and came out at the end of it with the 'breathtaking shock' of an 'amazingly energetic, brilliantly precise, and moving performance.' In her Schechner found 'a musician, a dancer, an actress . . . she trilled her voice, shaped tiny telling gestures, extended her backbone and neck and curled her toes so that all of her from the top of her head to the bottom of her feet was in the performance.'

In the last ten years of her life, she was cut off from her group, Bohurupee, and from her family. The accumulating losses culminated in her falling prey to cancer, keeping her bedridden for nearly a year and a half before her death on 24 May 1989. And yet those last few years were years of emancipated thinking and creativity, as she wrote plays and articles spelling out her doubts, fears, concerns, and commitments, centring on women. The project that had begun with *Aparajita* matured in her later works, both as actress and director, as she worked on roles that were manifestations of woman as actress, as working mother, as housewife discovering her individual identity, as lonely old woman, cut off from her children, happily settled elsewhere. She rarely had the supporting cast that she needed or the scenic resources that could have given her conceptions the space they required. But the mind moved unfalteringly and resolutely, as she tried to read herself as woman—left to/by herself for the first time—in dialogues with the characters she conceived/played.

Sujata, the central character of Mahasweta Devi's *Mother of 1084,* and Binodini, the late nineteenth century Bengali actress known through her widely read autobiography, were two of her favourite interlocutors. She left unfinished (the manuscript mysteriously lost) a play in which Binodini steps out of the past to challenge and question a current-day actress as she makes up for her evening performance, raising doubts about the supposed strides made by women since her time.

Dakghar

Aparajita

In the 43 years of my acting career, I have handled the widest possible range of characters from a domestic help to a Queen, and every time I have been acutely conscious of the obligation to speak every bit of the dialogue with the value it deserved. That is what any sensitive actor or actress would try to do anyway.

Then I came to my one woman performance, *Aparajita*—the undaunted—quite a challenge for me. An ordinary woman from a middle-class home, with little education, speaks directly to the audience through the length of the play, and yet not as a monologue. There is a series of telephone calls, and she takes advantage of them to confide in the audience and open up page after page from the story of her life. Stuck in the cribbed space of her dependency and her home, she needs a job desperately, to escape that space. That is why she waits for a telephone call. I act 18 roles in this play, a cross-section of society from the richest to the poorest—boys, men, women, beggars and philosophers. I brought all my acting experience into play to create this drama enacted between a helpless and yet optimistic young woman, and the narrow space in which society held her prisoner. She dreams of becoming an actress and making a living through that. As a child in school, she had been complimented on her acting talent, and that is when the dream had taken root—a dream that led through a career in acting to love and marriage and a home. The dream comes to naught, and at the end of it all, she tells the audience: 'I had hoped I'd be able to invite you to a theatre you'd have liked. But I'm sorry I can't.' The choice left to her is to look for a customer on the street. She does go out, but one never knows what she'll do once she's out there—in that other space where a cruel society drives her. When I tell all this to my audience, they are disturbed out of their space of contentment—and there I touch fulfilment. There have been several young women who have come and thanked me for what I've done for them. The space of communication that the actress creates between herself and her audience, her *sahridaya* clientele, is one that allows for a critical interpretation of the space of living that lies outside. Within the space that she dominates all the while that she is on stage, the actress tends to offer to her audience an awareness that should serve them in their struggle to understand and master the space outside—the mastery in the microcosm ensuring mastery over the macrocosm. As the actress feels her own mastery over her own space—a mastery determined by both skill and conscience—she feels in herself the power to cast her spell over the space of daily living. Even as she feels her word and action striking into the conscience of the spectator, the *chaitanyodaya* in the audience illuminates her too in the process; as the meaning of the words moves and stirs in the space within her, she herself crosses into yet another level of *chaitanya*.

Tripti Mitra

Sutarang

Pterodactyl

Hajar Churashir Ma

Raktakarabi

Utpal Dutt

Born in Barishal (now in Bangladesh), Utpal Dutt (1929-93) all his life claimed that he had been born in Shillong, a picturesque hill station up in north-eastern India—one of the many colourful myths that he conjured up to make himself somewhat larger than life, like the theatre that he always preferred to the more limitedly realistic models that he found dominating the scene when he entered it. There was nothing, however, in his beginnings in theatre in his college days—in a college run by a Belgian Jesuit mission in Calcutta—when he played in selected scenes from *Romeo and Juliet* and *Macbeth* and *Richard III*, to indicate the direction that his own theatre would take. In 1947 he found his 'guru'—Geoffrey Kendal, touring India, with a small company, in the late forties, playing Shakespeare and Shaw and Goldsmith, mainly to school audiences. Later in life he would dedicate his voluminous treatise in Bengali on the social sensibility of Shakespeare to Kendal, with the words: 'Dear Geoff, please permit me to dedicate this book to you. I cannot help it because you taught me what little I know of Shakespeare and have left me no other way of paying old debts.'

His life with the strolling Kendals lasted 'from August 1947 to the end of 1948, and again from February 1953 to the end of 1954—a long time, touring India and Pakistan, being beaten and kicked,' as Dutt told me in an interview, in which he said: 'Right from my childhood, right from the beginning, I had wanted my theatre *here*. I joined the Kendals to learn the theatre, and then did a few plays on my own, and they were in English, because I had learnt to act in English. But there's no sense in a production that will run for three nights! And those who came to see these plays knew the language less than us, and they would sit through *Twelfth Night* with grim determination writ on their faces. They were there to see Shakespeare, no nonsense! After a few experiences like these, we decided to give up. For, after all, the theatre is for audiences—Craig's words, "The theatre has always been, and will always be for the people . . .”

‘What I have brought over from my experiences in the English language theatre is the professional approach, discipline. That’s how we had learnt it—rising early and getting into the strictest routine of exercises and rehearsals—it was different only when we were travelling. I think I have been able to bring this method into my work in the theatre. And this is the professional approach. I am in violent disagreement with those who talk too much about ideas and idealism and would brand any actor who asks for money as a careerist, for the simple reason that the Kendals were ten times more serious than these people with their million and one ideals, and that because they were professional. No actor with the Kendals had any spare time; at all hours he was at the beck and call of the stage manager. Yet this discipline never became drudgery, for you knew everyone there loved the theatre, everyone knew that this was essential.’

Drawing on this exposure/experience, he would eventually—in 1959—take over Minerva Theatre, one of the city’s oldest surviving theatre ‘houses’, on a long lease and set up a regular company housed in it—a departure from the more familiar local model of the ‘houseless’ group without a theatre of its own! But between his stints with the Kendals and his ‘professional’ phase—or maybe ‘semiprofessional’, for Dutt and his company never earned enough from the theatre to live off it, and were compelled to supplement their income—there was a phase of radical experimentation in more senses than one, with the opportunity and challenge of performing to large audiences (stretching from five to ten thousand at a time) at political gatherings in rural settings.

Dutt’s first significant directorial experiment was a modern dress version of Shakespeare’s *Julius Caesar* in 1949, for the group Amateur Shakespeareans. A contemporary review noted: ‘Producing *Julius Caesar* in modern dress is not in itself a novel idea, the contemporary applications being obvious. Yet this performance contained several ingenious features. An extremely effective example was that Brutus’s and Antony’s funeral speeches were delivered over the radio, to an audience of conspirators, at first jubilant, then increasingly apprehensive. The battle scenes, to a background of machine-gun fire, possessed a coherence, difficult to achieve otherwise . . . The Caesareans were naturally portrayed as Fascists. As Caesar himself, Ellis Abraham, in hat and overcoat, recalled the early Hitler, though behaving with a dignity normally foreign to that gentleman; a deft performance . . . If the Fascist angle commands assent, portraying the conspirators as Socialists and Communists is more questionable. A better parallel to these reactionary Senatorial oligarchs would be the plot of Hitler's generals in 1944. Still, accepting the convention it was capably carried out. As the "noblest Roman of them all", Utpal Dutt played Brutus with distinction, especially in the scene where the conspiracy is launched, where a tormented Central European of the Kafka period hinted at the idealist shortly to be crushed in the world of dirty politics.'

The group led by Dutt, initially known as The Amateur Shakespeareans, was renamed the Little Theatre Group in 1950, and moved to productions in Bengali. Real popular success came with *Angaar* in 1959—at the Minerva Theatre, where for the first time one of the Calcutta-based non-professional groups had turned semi-professional with a theatre of its own. The first bunch of plays at Minerva, that included *Angaar, Ferari Fouj*, *Titash* and *Kallol* were marked by spectacle, sensation, violence—and what Dutt would later describe as 'the bold finish.' *Angaar* closed on a coalmine getting slowly flooded, with a band of trapped miners going under, with Tapas Sen's lighting out of cans with holes, flung on a canvas in the rear, supported by a piece of haunting music by Ravi Shankar, building it up to sheer panic. The major part of *Kallol*, set against the rebellion of the Indian ratings of the Royal Indian Navy in 1946, was played out on the deck of a ship that occupied the stage, its hull dominating the forestage, and the deck with its gun-turret at a considerable height. *Kallol* made a savage criticism of the Congress, the party in power in 1965, when it was premiered, charging it with betrayal of the revolutionary sailors and responsibility for their massacre at the hands of the British army. The ruling party hit back by arresting Dutt and detaining him without trial in the Presidency Jail. That became the excuse for most of the newspapers to stop carrying advertisements for *Kallol*. The performances continued, with a vigorous publicity campaign that flooded the city with handbills and plastered the city over with posters of all sizes, countermanding the black-out by the Press.

Released in March 1966, Dutt did a series of documentary plays at Minerva—on the US role in Vietnam and the heroic resistance by the Vietnamese; on the peasant revolt raging at the time in Naxalbari in north Bengal; and on Black Power revolutionaries studying the great Scottsboro trial. Meanwhile, Dutt had joined the Naxalite movement, going underground in November 1967, when an arrest warrant was issued in his name. After a cat and mouse game with the police, he was arrested in Bombay in early 1968, where he had turned up for the shooting of the Ivory-Merchant film, *The Guru*, in which he played the protagonist. He was released after a short stay in prison, on the intervention of his American producers. As Dutt writes, 'The government of West Bengal the same evening broadcast over the radio that I had signed a paper abjuring politics. It was a white lie, of course. I had merely endorsed what the film company had written. But it pleased me no end to note that the government thought it so important to try and demolish my reputation, proving they were afraid of it. There are certain individuals who pretend not to understand what actually happened and declare that I should have continued to live in prison. I have never believed in this kind of Gandhian self-torture. If given a reasonable chance to escape prison, I believe it should be seized at once.'

However Dutt rationalized the 'undertaking' that the government flaunted, the Little Theatre Group split and disintegrated on the issue. For a couple of years Dutt floundered, thrown out of the Minerva Theatre that had become identified with the LTG.

In the 1968-69 season, Dutt took his first professional assignment in the jatra, the popular traditional theatre-in-the-round carried by twenty-odd touring companies to the remotest parts of eastern India. After decades of contemptuous disregard from the urban theatregoer, the jatra was coming into a new respectability, when Dutt wrote and directed *Rifle*, with Panchu Sen, the great jatra actor, playing a rugged peasant, a departure from the regal roles with which his admirers associated him, premiering on 23 September 1968. In the years 1968-82, Dutt wrote and directed seventeen *palas* (as the jatra plays are called) for the professional jatra companies, enjoying himself thoroughly in handling a different breed of excellent actors and actresses, trained in a more flamboyant style, with its stops and rhythms set to a different code altogether.

As he discovered the potentials of the jatra, and knew that he would never have again a theatre of his own where he would have the freedom to play with all the available means and devices and technology of the modern theatre, he toyed with the idea of taking the jatra up as his own form.

Beginning from scratch, the first group that Dutt formed after the break-up of LTG and the dissociation from the Minerva Theatre was, significantly enough, a jatra company—the Vivek Jatra Samaj (*Vivek* translating as 'conscience'). Initially, there was the idea of having two parallel groups—the Vivek Jatra Samaj, performing in the round to large gatherings outside the big cities, and the People's Little Theatre carrying on in the proscenium.

But it was the People's Little Theatre that survived, and the Jatra Samaj that died a natural death, dogged by its failure to cope with too many organizational handicaps and the absence of a company of actors with the skills that the jatra called for. It was the immediate success of *Tiner Talwar* ['The Tin Sword', premiered 12 August 1971] that ensured a second run for Dutt. Set in late nineteenth century Calcutta, and rooted in the life of a professional theatre company, one of the first to emerge in the city, *Tiner Talwar* touched on several issues, including those of theatre responding to resurgent nationalism, the first generation of actresses, an Eliza Doolittle–Professor Higgins situation played out between a director and an actress, the old patronage system impinging upon theatre, and a whole range of theatre relationships, adding up to what director Satyadev Dubey described as an 'existential' view of theatre. The jatra, which retained for long several stylistic features and conventions of the late nineteenth century Bengali theatre, had provided Dutt with insights into that declining tradition that he could put to brilliant use in *Tiner Talwar*, which, in the plays within the play, re-created the characteristic acting modes and musical traditions of the period in which it was located, and set them against a later-day theatre technology involving revolving discs, rostra, illumination, etc. to set a specific period in Bengal's cultural history in perspective, and raise issues of gender, colonialism, protest, revolt, and the social function of culture. The performance as a whole moved with great theatric dynamism from realistic acting to period histrionics, to singing, to rugged farce, to melodrama, making the transitions along a groundwork of irony.

The next PLT hit, *Barricade*, premiered 25 December 1972, set in Germany in the early thirties, with the Communists fighting one of their last street battles against the Nazis who would soon take over, and the liberal democrats taking their stand at the barricades alongside the Communists, provided audiences in Emergency India with a point of reference for the proto-fascist conditions prevailing in India. While the audience, otherwise held in leash by the draconian laws of the Emergency, could enjoy the freedom of recognition and celebration of the recognition in laughter and applause, there was no way the perpetrators of the Emergency could take a stand against *Barricade*, for any such attempt to scuttle it would have been acknowledgement on their part of the relevance of the work. But *Duswapner Nagari* ['Nightmare City', premiered 16 April 1974], the second play of what later came to be called the Emergency Trilogy, came in for organized resistance, instigated by the authorities—in the form of sieges of the theatres, and attacks on the cast by musclemen—culminating in a sedition suit filed by the police.

The radical phase in Dutt's theatre came to a close with the coming to power of a Leftist United Front in the state of West Bengal. Dutt's theatre seemed to have lost its purpose with the Left comfortably settled in power. The actors in his group, too, were settling down to a cushy, official kind of theatre. Dutt was compelled to take on the big roles—something that he had resolutely resisted for years—in a desperate endeavour to keep the group running. He was losing health fast in his last years, and was yet capable of playing the lead in plays like *Ajker Shahjahan* and *Danrao Pathikbar*, holding the otherwise loose and wandering productions together with his own individual performance. As playwright, director, and actor, he remained imaginative, innovative and creative till the end, but at the helm of a group of mostly indifferent and careless actors, he could rarely achieve what he hoped to, with his texts loaded with political meaning and vision.

There was this old farce by Michael Madhusudan Dutt which we produced in 1954 and which we still play occassionally. The part I play is that of a filthy old rustic lord, whose indiscriminate womanizing leads him finally to an ambush by angry masked peasants, who pretend to be ghosts—much like Falstaff's predicament in *Merry Wives of Windsor*. I felt, one should not try subtleties in a loud farce of this nature, and decided to abandon all attempts at identification and to play it straight as great fun, relying on every slapstick trick I could think of. I chose a bald wig with a stubborn wisp of white hair standing in a desert. I took no responsibility for that dirty old man's own point of view, and what he thought of his insatiable sexual exploits and of the torture of peasants for rent that the playwright opens the play with.

Everywhere the audience roared with laughter, citymen and workers, enjoying the antics of a monster they have never seen. And then we went to a village to play before peasants and stunned silence greeted the first bout of horseplay. These peasants were seeing something which is their daily life—being evicted for non-payment of rent, being whipped, their women seduced by pimps of the lord. They were not laughing with me at my part, they were hostile, balefully looking on at their class-enemy, hating me. It was no laughing matter to them.

I believe it was this miasma of hostility that drove me to a defensive pose. I had already fumbled with a couple of lines, because the laughs had not come in their usual places. I felt the hatred out in the dark field outside, and wanted to defend the part I was playing, wanted to defend myself, and assert the evil lord's own logic to hit back at the grim faces. And the part changed—then and there—the horseplay disappeared, the slapsticks were abandoned. If the audience was not going to laugh with me, they would see how terrible their adversary could be. The seduction of the peasant's wife was no longer funny, but the lord's maniacal revenge of his class-enemy. At the end of the performance, we felt we had supped full of horror. We had misread the play and my part. We had underestimated the dramatist, ignoring the significance of the first scene, the economic basis of the lord's lusty

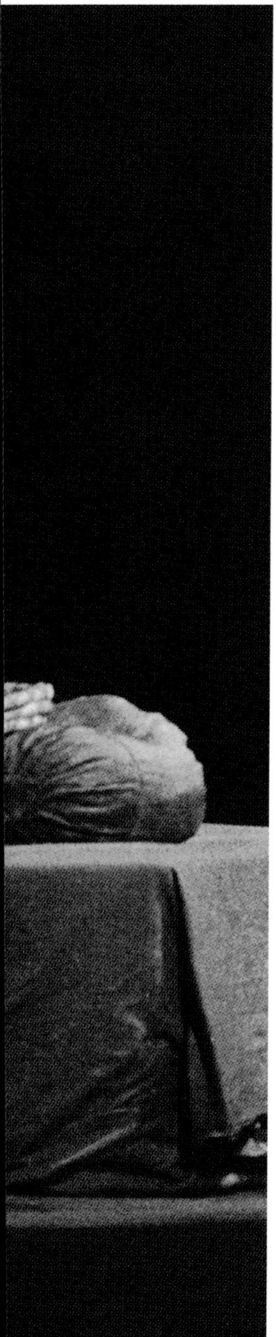

Buro Shaliker Ghadey Ron

doings. Sex was his way of getting back at these dishonest peasants who cheated him of what was, to him, his due by British dispensation. (He refers in the play to the East India Company's pressure.) The play was not a farce at all, it was a frightening chronicle. And my purely external appproach to the part, merely interpreting it as a clown, was shaken, by the audience reacting on the basis of their own experience of life.

This is what the Audience does to the contradictions of the theatre. They bring their actual life-experience to bear upon the stage. They react to plays from the standpoint of their own personal sufferings and have the strength to alter the values enshrined in a performance. The audience is the link between life and theatre.

During the performance in question, I was forced to share the lord's view of life for a short time. I saw life and his enemies as he saw them.

And I also felt, at final curtain, that I had seen hell, the devious inner working of an oppressor's mind.

Manusher Adhikarey

Another time, playing Liebowitz, the lawyer, in my play *The Rights of Man* (on the Scottsboro Trial, 1931), I was engrossed in the ideals of the man, his unrelenting fight for the rights of his black client, Haywood Patterson, defying the hysterical white Alabama mob. Right through rehearsals I was trying to build up this idealistic lawyer, refusing to compromise in any way whatsoever. But that was not the part I had written, and it needed the first-night audience to break down this one-sided and false picture of an airy idealist, and bring out a shrewd, earthy professional lawyer, who knew every dirty trick the prosecution was likely to play and played it better. The way the audience greeted the first cross-examination of a false witness—a roguish, sympathetic laugh, that seemed to wink and say: we know you are tricking the man into perjury, but well done, only crooks can fight crooks! This kept on, as the long court scene wound on. The audience, from its experience, did not believe that honest lawyers exist anywhere. But they wanted Liebowitz to play dirty, because you could not fight a racist mob any other way.

I confess, everything I had complacently built up during the ten days of rehearsal, the over-simple hero, collapsed when the audience acted upon it. My Liebowitz became as devious a trickster as the prosecutor Tom Knight, taking free recourse to illegal and extra-legal methods to win his point, browbeating timid witnesses, being sycophantic to tough ones and then tripping them over a minor slip somewhere in their evidence, ruthlessly grilling a lame half-witted boy and a helpless prostitute. Even my walk changed, from a stride to a mischievous shuffle. And from the second night, I wore a monocle, which could be polished endlessly to the discomfort of the witnesses.

. . . In my struggle with the part of Liebowitz, almost unknown to me, I had sought a mechanical solution to the problem of Good and Bad, and had thought of Liebowitz almost as a Messiah. The constant factor—audience—rectified this process, and I was forced into the negative features of the man. The resultant Liebowitz, I make bold to say, was more human, more wholesome, more complete. And this happened to me in a play written by myself. All the elements of Liebowitz's cunning and even brutality were there in the play all the time, staring at me. And yet in rehearsals I had moderated them to the kind pronouncements of a latter-day sermon on the mount.

I had been thinking about Documentary Theatre from 1960, mainly influenced by Piscator's writings. I believe that the most effective political propaganda is propaganda that places facts and truths at the disposal of the audience. It took me three days and nights to write *Manusher Adhikarey* in 1961, for with the Court proceedings of the Scottsboro trials before me I had a script right there, and I knew that it would be disastrous to add anything to it. If I merely presented the facts as they really were, I knew I could tear to pieces all the myths that shroud the reality of the American way of life, with its deceptions and pretences.

When I produced it in 1968, I added a Prologue and an Epilogue based on the Detroit uprising in June 1968 and connected the play to the latest historical trend in the Black Revolution.

Utpal Dutt

Leniner Dak

Melodrama? Yes, but melodrama is a comparative term. In the battlefield, where the question of India's freedom is being decided, nothing is melodrama; everything is commonplace. In a way, *Hamlet* is the loudest melodrama ever written, whereas in a middle-class drawing room anything more assertive than 'Good morning' and 'How are you' could sound melodramatic.

Utpal Dutt

Apart from the fact that theatre has to represent truthfully the appalling violence that we have to live with every day, with Hiroshima, Vietnam, and the Star Wars project, violence in the arts also enables the creator to break down his audience's alienation, to startle him, to awaken his dulled senses. Bertolt Brecht called this a technique of 'erstaunen', stunning the audience by a violent scene in the play . . . Violence also broadens our vision of human character, the unexpected twists and turns and rages of human beings. The bourgeois always wants his characters cut-and-dried, humdrum and logical. He is afraid of uncharted passions and sudden changes.

. . .

Violence in the theatre has discovered psychological depths of the human mind that destroys the bourgeois concept of man as a fully-researched type. Now influenced by this bourgeois way of thinking, many of us pretend to be bored or offended by violence. Actually we are startled by the things man can do to other men, or that we can do to other men. We resist this self-discovery with hypocrisy. Violence in the arts shatters this hypocrisy. We live in an era of all-pervasive political violence. Streets resound, in at least a half of the world, with political demonstrations and police brutality—and political gangsters who once threw fire-bombs in Calcutta to enforce a general strike that no one observed.

. . .

What is modern theatre to do? Cushion the audience against reality with false promises of peace? Or equip it with consciousness? Tell lies of class peace, the Indian Utopia? The twentyfirst century? Or confront the audience with reality? From its very origin, the theatre has sought to destroy illusions of class peace and social peace, and comfortable lies about man being a tame and domesticated animal.

It will be our endeavour to re-discover history, which has been distorted and raped by hirelings of the bourgeois, and tell the story of the patriotic communist, accused of waging war against the King-Emperor, not defending himself, but thundering counter-accusations from the dock at

Kanpur and Meerut. It does not matter that the leaders made mistakes. The communist is historically the only revolutionary. He alone struggles today for the liberation of the masses and therefore he alone is justified by history. He alone is capable of liberating Asia, Africa and Latin America, and in him is summarized the heroism of the Chinese People's Liberation Army and the African guerrilla.

. . . I have tried, in the theatre and the Yatra, to select stories of revolutionaries of the immediate past and show the continuity of struggle, from Surya Sen to the modern proletariat. I have written and produced *Kallol*, *Rifle* (about the Bengal revolutionaries of the early thirties; I drew the story forward to 1947 to show that the collaborators of 1930 had become congress ministers in 1947), *Jallianwalabag* (about the Punjab revolutionaries), *Storm Clouds* (Baisakhi Megh—also about Bengal rebels), *Kripan* (about the Ghadr party in the Punjab and the mutiny of the 23rd Indian cavalry) . . . To be unaware of the present state of class struggle, the specific political demands of the proletariat at this given time, is to land in quixotism, quite unrelated to the actual struggle of the masses, and create plays that will parade revolution in the abstract, merely as a philosophical concept, and may perhaps influence a coterie of petty-bourgeois intellectuals, but will remain abstruse and dead to the revolutionary classes, a bigger waste of time being unimaginable. A revolutionary theatre that does not aim at the revolutionary masses is a ridiculous contradiction in terms. To us, the truth is concrete. It relates to a specific time, specific place and specific stage of the revolution.

Utpal Dutt

Tiner Talwar

Tiner Talwar

Barricade

Barricade ran into rough waters. Gangs of heavily-armed and drink-crazed rogues would regularly visit us backstage and warn us not to say anything against the Lady. We would counter it with a simple argument: The play is about Hitler, why does that hurt you? Do you then admit that the cap fits, that you are Nazis? They usually left after that.

But with *Nightmare City*, a play about the murder of communists in Calcutta by Congress gangsters, and the way the police, the press and the so-called Congress youth leaders co-operate in the task, roused the enemy to real effort, especially because of the massive crowds which besieged the box-office every day. They planned to suppress it.

To the Star Theatre where we were scheduled to play of an evening, they sent an army of the worst criminals of north Calcutta, armed to the teeth, and about noon time they broke into the theatre, where only the stage crew was setting up. The exponents of Indira democracy beat up the unarmed crewmen, smashed our sets and burnt a part of them. Then they blockaded every door and waited for us.

When I arrived at about 3.30 p.m. I found a screaming mob, yelling, 'Go back, go back!' and a large contingent of armed policemen guarding them. I tried to get past the mob whereupon they pushed and pummelled me across the road. I saw Tapas Sen, India's foremost expert of lighting, being knocked down by a bunch of thugs. Sabita Banerjee, actress, was dragged by her hair down the road. A few people, living close by, protested and the police, hitherto soporific, suddenly charged them with the butts of their rifles. Clearly, we would have to tangle with armed policemen if we tried to go in. We left the place.

I must record here the courage of the local residents who formed a knot around my wife, Sova Sen, and protected her from the mob.

We had to go on playing *The Nightmare City*. We could not let them get away with an outrage like that.

. . . The Chief Minister said, 'Political plays will naturally be dealt with politically.' To break up a show by violence was Mr. Siddhartha Ray's conception of political dealing.

And, as usual, the CPI(M) members of South Calcutta came out of hiding to guard the next show at a southern theatre. They barricaded both ends of the street and checked tickets there. They kept the street before the theatre entirely free of pedestrians. The play went on, with angry bursts of bombs at a distance. We kept playing all over Bengal, changing the name of the play when the Magistrate gave trouble. All the same, my diary says, this play alone was attacked 14 times, and of them, in 13 cases the gangsters were beaten off by communist guards.

Then, Mr. Bibhuti Chakrabarty, Deputy Commissioner, Detective Department, filed sedition charges against us.

Section 124-A provides for a maximum sentence of 15 years' hard labour. Also, the manuscript of the play was seized and while the case was in trial, we could not perform the play.

In court we submitted a long list of witnesses we would call to prove that *Nightmare City* was a truthful record of what was actually happening. The list included all the top officers of the police and one Governor who had in articles in the press from time to time inadvertently admitted to numerous crimes; one officer let slip that torture of prisoners in police-stations had assumed the proportions of a scandal; an Inspector General had virtually confessed that the murder of policemen in Calcutta should be attributed to union rivalries and not to the Naxalites or the CPI(M). We intended to confront these officers with their own statements in print. Understandably, the prosecutor began postponing further hearings.

And then Mrs. Gandhi and her clique, with the help of their playboy Siddhartha Ray, tore up the Constitution of India, and thus committed high treason. They proclaimed an Emergency during peace and swiftly put all the opposition leaders in prison, vindicating what the communists had been saying all along—the vicious little glorified village called New Delhi is the enemy of all Indian nations; it is a crude weapon in the hand of the ruling class, and the day the bosses find their own constitution is hindering them, they will unhesitatingly abolish it.

Utpal Dutt

Danrao Pathikbar

BAR
OPEN

Ballad for the Nightmare City

You'll malign my beloved still?
You'll still call her depraved?
There she stands in rags, plastered over with dust.
You charge her with having traded her body.
Still I adore her face rent with compassion.
She is my night's respite, my day's delight,
As she wipes my sweat away with her hardened hands—
Calcutta, my darling city.

The curling smoke veils her face,
The signs on the walls marking it with lines.
Her tresses sprawl down the black pitch street,
And still an empress, tattooed with all the filth and slush,
The concrete mansions her ring finger,
With my name glowing on her ring, flushed with neon lights,
My gifts of a necklace of electric diamonds sparkling around her neck.
Calcutta, my darling city.

My beloved stands naked today, a ravished Draupadi,
Torn with hunger, her chest parched with thirst.
The Kauravas have left her stripped of her beauty, her youth, her dignity.
The sink their teeth into her flesh, they guzzle her blood.
Her face streaming with blood, she shakes with rage,
She assumes the warrior's stance, and plunges into never-ending battle—
Calcutta, my darling city . . .
You called my Calcutta a nightmare,
Called it the Terrible City of Processions.
Yes, Calcutta will always be a nightmare to the rulers,
Her processions a terror to the oppressors.

Calcutta defies the darkness that blinds her for a moment,
For she sees the easterly glow of the tomorrow beyond,
As she waits for the dawn with a heart full of hate,
Waiting for the bells that ring the deathknell for the oppressors.

Utpal Dutt

Duswapner Nagari

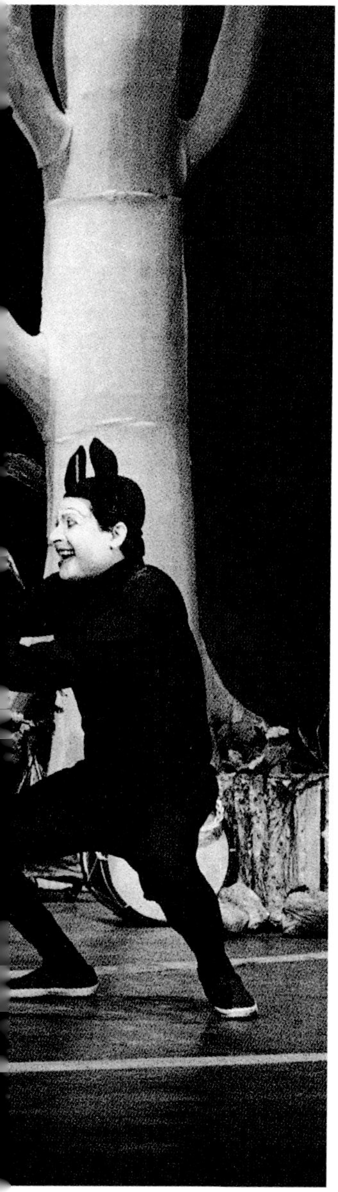
Chaitali Rater Swapna

The forest in *A Midsummer Night's Dream* is not merely trees, creepers, leaves and flowers. It is inhabited by fairies, who are not exactly the flying fairies of the fairy-tales glowing with the gold wands held in their hands. They are just as vicious as men. The forest represents a visual image of the human subconscious, objectifying the meaningless fears and tensions that cripple a man's mind in his boyhood. Hence the forest is beautiful and terrible at the same time, like childhood memories. In *A Midsummer Night's Dream* Shakespeare attempts a first treatment of the centuries long history of the dark forces in the human mind that would surface in the scene of the Walpurgisnacht in Goethe's *Faust*.

The forest represents a crystallization of man's loneliness and alienation. The four lovers who run away from society do not find peace in the forest; they experience a more bitter hatred against one another, conflict, and going round and round in the dark to the point of utter exhaustion.

And Bottom becomes a donkey. Man has obviously turned society to a state where 'godlike' man (in Hamlet's words) is turning into a stupid animal devoid of feeling and conscience. While Bottom literally turns into a donkey in the forest, the long process of men turning into donkeys has been continuing in the minds of men for a long time. Bottom's apppearance as half donkey and half man is the ultimate image of the social alienation of man. Bottom was the model for Ionesco's man turning into rhinoceros.

Utpal Dutt

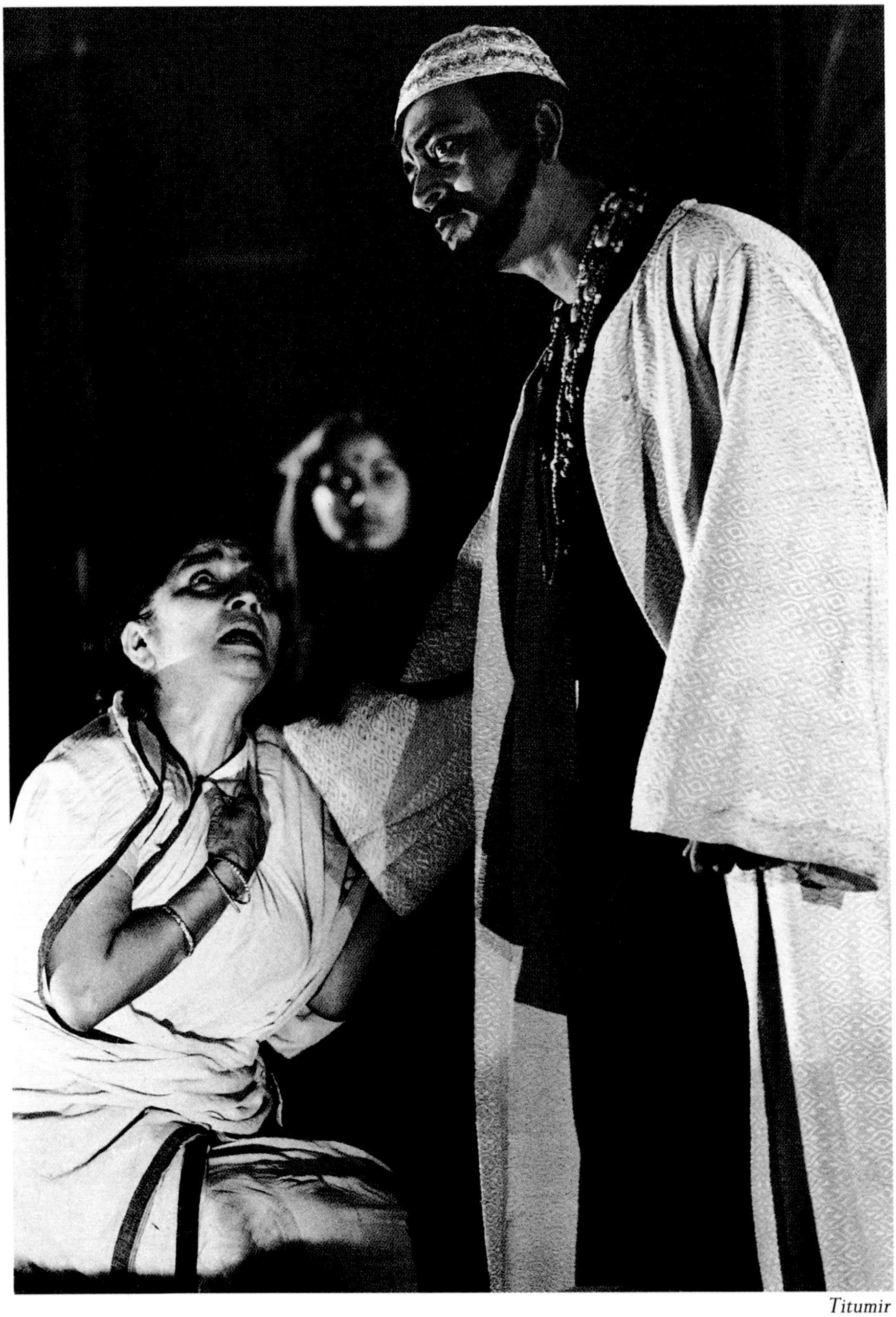

Titumir

Ajitesh Bandyopadhyay

Dark, with chiselled features, and, at nearly six foot and a half, unusually tall for a Bengali, Ajitesh Bandyopadhyay (1933-83) was quite literally a towering presence on the stage. In his speech and intonation, in his gait and stance, he bore the unmistakable mark of a man from the frontiers. His birthplace was the dry, hot, rocky, mining district of Barddhaman, close to the neighbouring state of Bihar, with a tribal belt spread across the border of the two states. In his strong, rugged, virile appearance, and his fast, staccato speech, his voice low and confident, he seemed to exude the character of a native—quite unlike the urban middle class persona that has dominated the Bengali theatre all along. Naive and imprudent, he could charm women and young people in general with his innocence and passion, and put the wary and the calculating on their guard. A stern disciplinarian and an administrator who insisted on monitoring every little detail of an organization or a production whenever he was in overall charge, he probably demanded too much from his colleagues, and hence could not count for too long on their loyalty. The very few who stuck to him till the end adored him almost to the point of worship.

A cardholding member of the Communist Party in the late fifties, Bandyopadhyay lived in a slum in a northern suburb of Calcutta and, for a spell, in the one-room local party office itself. He taught at a neighbourhood school for his living, served his Party obligations with exemplary dedication (his duties included going round the locality in a rickshaw, campaigning for the Party or one of the causes projected by the Party, addressing the people over a hand-held microphone), and was active as director and actor and secretary in the local unit of the Indian People's Theatre Association, before he started his own independent theatre group, Nandikar, in 1960. In his IPTA days, he wrote and directed *Santhal Bidroha*, a play valorizing a tribal revolt in 1855-56, in the loud, militant style that was so characteristic of the IPTA at the time.

A dedicated Party activist as long as he retained his Party membership, he had his differences with the Party leadership from time to time. In one of these encounters, he confronted Pramod Dasgupta, the Stalinist strong man of Communist politics in the state of West Bengal. At a meeting of party activists, Dasgupta had made an appeal to the party's theatre workers to put on poster plays for the Party's election campaign. Bandyopadhyay refused. He said that he would rather go around, visiting the voters at their homes, address street corner meetings, accompany and guide voters to the polling centres, work as a polling agent for the Party, and contribute in all possible ways to the campaign. Doing a rabble-rouser quickie for the Party at election time was not his idea of Party service. His differences with the party's cultural establishment came to a head when he produced his adaptation of Pirandello's *Six Characters in Search of an Author* in 1961. In the local Party circles Pirandello was considered an out and out Fascist, and a Communist had no business staging the work of a Fascist!

Nandikar, the theatre group that he led from 1960 to 1977, was founded on 29 June 1960 as a branch of the IPTA. In 1961, the group disaffiliated itself from the IPTA and became an independent entity. In its first few years, Nandikar produced a wide range of plays, most of them adaptations of European and American classics, most of them adapted by, and all of them directed by, Bandyopadhyay. Beginning with Ibsen's *Ghosts* (1960), he went on to do Tagore's *Char Adhyay* ['Four Chapters'] (1961), Chekhov's *The Cherry Orchard* (1964), Wesker's *Roots* (1966), Pirandello's *Henry IV* (1966), Ionesco's *Lesson* (1968), culminating in *Tin Paisar Pala* (1969), his adaptation of Brecht's *Threepenny Opera*. In his often controversial adaptations of most of the plays, Bandyopadhyay transplanted the original texts to situations more familiar to his audience. In the process, more often than not significant elements of the original text were either lost or diluted; but the play, in most cases totally indigenized, retained, in the spirit of the production, in the acting style, and in the scenography, the essence of the dramatic mode to which it belonged. As Bandyopadhyay explained in conversations, what he needed, in the absence of a clearly defined theatrical tradition, and in the context of the burden of a weird mix of the Victorian melodramatic hangover and halfhearted Stanislavskian practice, was an opportunity and the freedom to actually grapple with a wide range of living traditions, and texts that challenged both conventional morality and the more familiar modes of performance. With his repertoire of adaptations, too often criticized from both nationalist and indigenist and purist and authenticist positions, he brought to Bengali theatre and its audiences an awareness of theatric modes and possibilities that opened up the creative scope of Bengali theatre to a considerable extent.

In one of his finest productions *Jakhan Eka* [lit. 'When Alone,' from Wesker's *Roots*], a young working woman, living in the suburbs, 'enlightened' politically and socially by her communist boyfriend, is seen in her suburban, lower-middle-class home, waiting one long evening for the communist friend to visit her family for the first time. The family, joining her sceptically, only to be disappointed at the end, then turning on the woman sneeringly; while the young woman literally steps out of/beyond the open, skeletal structure of the household, and begins to explain it all to herself, till she realizes with a thrill that she has found a voice for herself, and for the first time in her life she is speaking her own text, with no quotes/repeats from what her communist boyfriend had 'lectured' at her! The sheer glory of that moment, of a plain-looking, unassuming little actress hitting a realization, and 'revealing' herself, lives on, in the memories of many viewers.

Tin Paisar Pala, Nandikar's greatest hit, broke away from the Bengali mainstream tradition of a theatre that privileged the well articulated use of the voice and facial expression over the expressive manipulation of the body—in its bold physicality, its celebration of the ugly and the vulgar, its shamelessly catchy tunes, its mockery of conventional morality, its critique of the institutions of law and order. In spite of, or maybe because of, the utterly disorganized and cluttered look of the performance, the theatre seemed to inhabit an open space, which could at ease incorporate and/or transform itself into segments of an elaborate and intricate urban underworld, set in Calcutta in the 1870s, the city slang and the costumes and pointed historical references providing its locus in time. More than the subtitles on slides, or those inscribed on posters carried across the stage by crudely dancing footmen, it was the songs and recitatives and the acting style that played with and stripped down the typicality of the acts associated with cops and robbers, beggars and whores; allowing the audience insights into the mechanism of games and strategies that wove them into a social system—though the system appeared less political than Brecht read it. Macheath, the bourgeois gangster, was considerably lumpenized, but retained the natural power that, as one of his not too particularly sympathetic critics acknowledged, 'could quell his henchmen with a look.'

Under his leadership, Nandikar had survived a major split in the group in 1966, when Bibhash Chakraborty left the group, with leading actress Maya Ghosh and six or seven others. But it could not survive the success of *Tin Paisar Pala*, which encouraged Bandyopadhyay to move into a regular theatre, performing four times every week. In the new dispensation, there was pressure on the group to produce more new plays, more popular stuff.. Bandyopadhyay chose *Bitangsha* (1971) an adaptation of *Arsenic and Old Lace*, which was a middling success, but the productions that followed did not have the directorial power that his earlier works had exuded. The group of part-time actors and actresses reeled under the pressure of the busy schedule; funds were running out fast: both Bandyopadhyay and Keya Chakrabarty, the lead actress of the company, had to take on all kinds of assignments to support themselves, since they had both thrown up their jobs to work full time for the group. With less time for rigorous rehearsals, the productions suffered. Bandyopadhyay, Chakrabarty and a few others were among the few who could maintain a decent level of acting; the rest faltered. Meanwhile Nandikar had thrown up a second director, Rudraprasad Sengupta, who made his debut with Anouilh's *Antigone* (1975), a flawed and wavering production, redeemed by brilliant performances by Bandyopadhyay as Creon, and Chakrabarty as Antigone; with Creon's cold authority, played with a steely sheen, creating its own ruthless logic against Antigone's all too vulnerable naivete.

Eased out of Nandikar, Bandyopadhyay founded his new group, Nandimukh, on 9 September 1977, and went on to produce two masterpieces, *Paap-Punya* [lit. 'Sin and Virtue,' from Tolstoy's *The Power of Darkness*, premiered 28 July 1978], and *Tetrishtama Janmadin* [lit. 'The Thirtythird Birthday,' from Pinter's *The Birthday Party*, premiered 16 June 1982]. In both the plays, his last two productions, he dealt with violence and the ethics of violence. He had lived through and suffered with the political violence of the seventies in Calcutta, in all its forms and manifestations; and the years had been agonizing for Bandyopadhyay at a more personal level, with a marriage on the rocks and the inevitable complications of settling down to a new relationship outside marriage, still a difficult proposition in Calcutta, and the hard chase for money to support his brothers, sisters, and the two families! Bandyopadhyay was straining at commercial assignments in the TV, in the Jatra, in popular cinema, the strain taking its daily toll on his health. The violence of it all went into the making of those last two productions, with violence shaping sexuality, authority, social and familial communication, and even the idioms that the characters speak in, and yet never quite exploding on the stage, stopping all so precariously just short of it.

He died—of sheer emotional and physical exhaustion—on 14 October 1983. Till a few days before the end he was contemplating new work in the Jatra—and Shakespeare's *The Tempest.*

Tin Paisar Pala

Q. You have acted in both *Bhalomanush*—'The Good Person of Szechuan'—and Anouilh's *Antigone*. Which of the two roles has attracted and inspired you more?

A. *Bhalomanush* is of course a far superior play, with a much greater scope. But for a little more than two thousand and five hundred years the character of Antigone has served as a legend to mankind. Every night I play Antigone I try to rise to the challenge of turning a legend into a living presence. The challenge in *Bhalomanush* is one of acting a man and a woman in the same play. Let's put it like this—the need to play *Bhalomanush* is like the need to breathe. But with Antigone, I can dream.

Tin Paisar Pala

Q. Who are you most indebted to, when it comes to theatre training and encouragement?

A. Ajitesh Bandyopadhyay, Ajitesh Bandyopadhyay and Ajitesh Bandyopadhyay.

Keya Chakrabarty

Bhalo Manush

Antigone

Antigone, the stage: Calcutta

Struck by a sudden failure of electricity,
Ajitesh-Creon and Keya-Antigone stop their dialogue,
To measure the darkness spread across the city's plain.

'Why is it so dark?'
Questions rise from an audience indistinguishable in one-
ness,
Till there are those who walk up right on to the stage

And set alight a few wax candles, their brief flames
Burning Creon's mantle, the fire fed by
Antigone who turns herself into the sacrificial butter!

Alokeranjan Dasgupta

Antigone

Nati Binodini

Bitangsha

Paap Punya

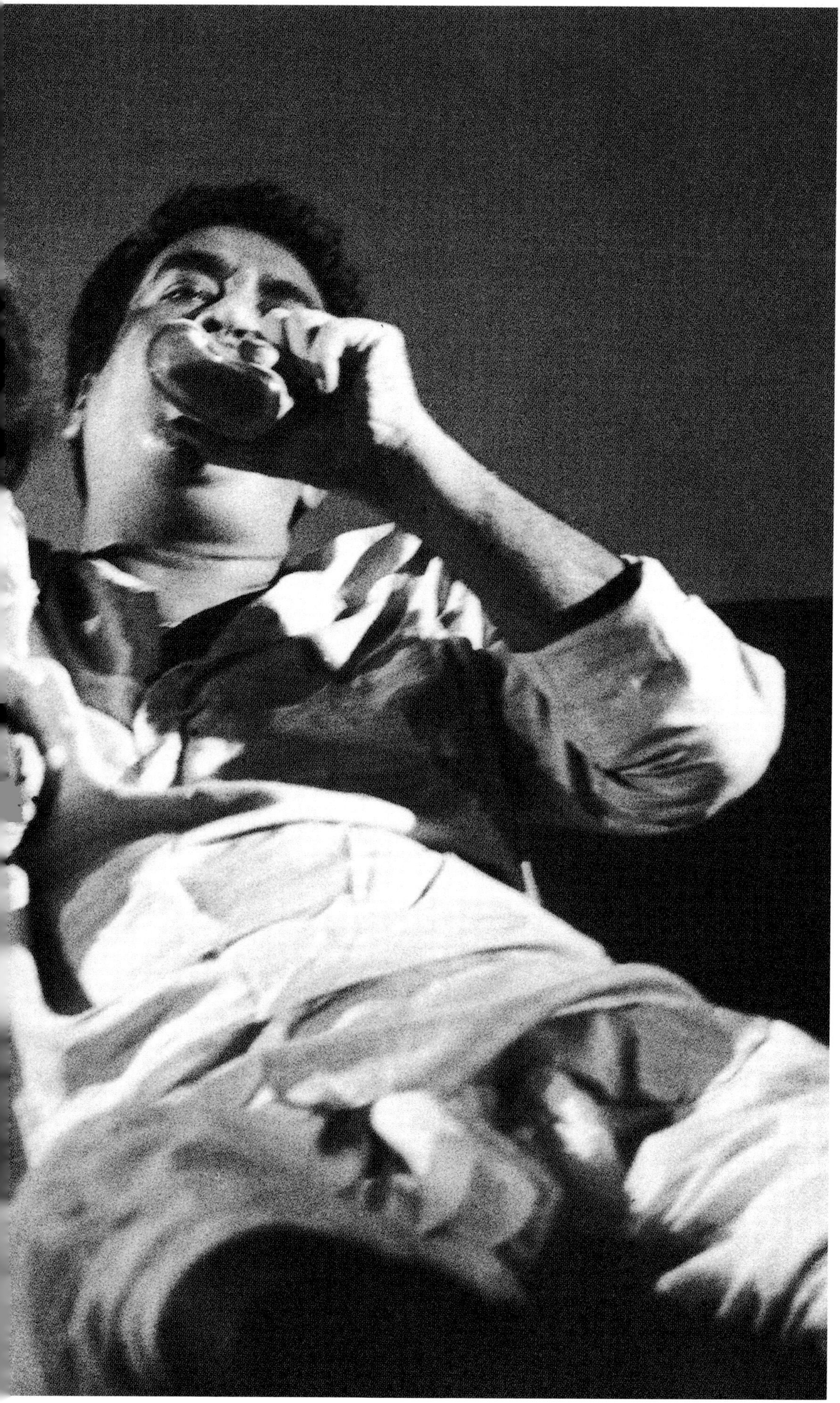

Paap Punya

Paap Punya

Seventies to the Nineties: An Overview

By the close of the sixties, most of the actor-directors who had dominated Bengali theatre for the preceding two decades had reached their peak and were already showing signs of exhaustion. Some of them were, of course, seeking new directions, some crashing in the process, some transforming themselves into new identities in the next decade. The mid-sixties and early seventies were marked by the emergence of a generation of new directors, who did not match the individual brilliance and mastery of Bijan Bhattacharya, Sombhu Mitra, Utpal Dutt and Ajitesh Bandyopadhyay at their best, but were able to extend the frontiers of Bengali theatre considerably. Political satire; musical plays (mainly biographical plays on singers and composers of an earlier period, offering scope for a lot of stage singing); documentary plays; adaptations of well-known European and American plays; treatment/exposures of immediate reality; street plays, and their more strident and blatantly propagandist variation, the poster plays; a more strongly physical mode geared to the intimate performing space; plays drawing on folk performing practices, being 'discovered' for the first time, were some of the new directions opening out.

There were four survivors from the earlier phase who broke fresh ground in 1965-75. Bijan Bhattacharya (1915-78), who had been the progenitor of the post-World War II Bengali theatre with his 1944 play *Nabanna* [which he co-directed with Sombhu Mitra for the Indian People's Theatre Association in 1944], hit on an indigenous 'epic theatre' form in his *Debigarjan* (1966) and *Garbhabati Janani* (1969), in which a slice of life representing a marginal, deprived community is elaborately conveyed through intimate, casual details to the point of suggesting a seamless, impregnable continuity, firmly entrenched in its structure of social relationships and beliefs, for over two-thirds of the play; till the cracks show in the last third, bringing to light the hidden forces, social and economic, that exploit the community and delude it into submission and acquiescence. The sudden exposure amounts to a seismic fissure that either erupts into revolutionary violence (as in *Devigarjan*) or rises to a quiet enlightenment/end of delusion (as in *Garbhabati Janani*).

Utpal Dutt had to recast and redefine his theatric style when at the turn of the decade he lost his theatre, the old Minerva Theatre that he had held on lease for a whole decade, and his old company, and had to begin again from scratch. The Little Theatre Group, in its Minerva days, had developed an exemplary skill (the credit goes primarily to lighting designer Tapas Sen) in improvising new technology—making use of readily available resources and objects and used and abandoned bric a brac—for spectacle; turning the stage to a coal mine being flooded with a band of miners getting drowned (Ravi Shankar's haunting score casting the necessary spell for the illusion of a mass of water rising steadily and ominously); or to the deck of a battleship, from where mutinous naval ratings fire salvos at the Admiral's flagship. Dutt had trained his LTG actors to a level of military discipline that enabled him to achieve flawless timing, precision and choreography in ensemble acting.

In the early seventies, left without a theatre of his own, Dutt had to give up the rich spectacularity of his Minerva productions, and settle for a different kind of dramaturgy, using a more manageable technique, even while retaining his mastery of stage space and visualization. His new group, People's Little Theatre, was basically a new assortment of actors, who came from different schools of acting. With far fewer performances and rehearsals, and the performances spread over a wide variety of 'stages,' often makeshift structures in the middle of a field, or small town theatres, PLT could never gear itself up to the productional finesse and efficiency of its earlier incarnation, LTG, and had to fall back on the individual talents of a few actors and actresses, with Dutt himself taking on leading roles. Dutt's continuing experimentation with theatric modes approached the Brechtian model, without ever quite chasing it.

Soon after the PLT had made its first impact with *Tiner Talwar*

(1971), a play on theatre in nineteenth century Calcutta, and an existential view of theatre at the same time, Asit Bose, one of its leading actors, split from the group to form the Calcutta People's Art Theatre. The CPAT came into its own with *Kolkatar Hamlet* (1973), after an indifferent version of Chekhov's *The Seagull* and a visually rich and ornate 'Elizabethan' exercise with Clemence Dane's *Will Shakespeare*, with Aparna Sen (now a leading film director and star) playing Mary Fitton, the Dark Lady of Shakespeare's sonnets, driving Shakespeare to kill Chris Marlowe! *Kolkatar Hamlet* brings Shakespeare's Hamlet to Calcutta in the seventies, with urban guerrillas clashing with the police and the representatives of the parliamentary Left, and getting tortured and killed in a losing battle. The urban guerrillas find a kindred soul in Hamlet who seeks a personal consummation in the violence with which they challenge State and Society. Bose showed that he had learnt his lessons from Dutt, and managed to convey the state of terror that held the city in thrall, in the sheer pace of the action, the transformation of stage space, the unexpected transitions from the farcic to the melodramatic to the discursive to the fantastic to the grimly naturalistic, allowing Death itself a presence in a political scenario; the shifting perspectives opening up a dream space halfway between the immediately real and the unreal.

In *Kolkatar Hamlet*, Bose showed a mastery of stage technology and scenography, a skill in the handling of an ensemble, that would soon be lost to theatre in Calcutta. Bose was to retreat from theatre a few years later, and the strain of survival, the struggle to keep a less-than-competent company together and to make it effective, was to take its toll of Dutt's energies.

Bose's split from the PLT was only one in a series of such splits from parent companies that had come to dominate the non-professional theatre scene in Calcutta in the early fifties. The first had taken place in late 1951, when Tulsi Lahiri, Kali Sarkar, Sabitabrata Datta and Geeta Dutta had broken off from Sombhu Mitra's Bohurupee. Initially, they joined Anandam, and produced Lahiri's

Banglar Mati; but they went on to form Rupakar, which, in the sixties and seventies, restored to Calcutta theatre its long lost tradition of a singing theatre that could cope with both comedy and period plays with equal ease and fun. Rupakar folded up in the seventies, with Datta moving over to the professional theatre, to make a hit of *Antony Kabiyal* (1966), in which he played the title role of a feringhee poet-singer in nineteenth century Calcutta, taking part in singing debates in public spaces, and coming to terms with the popular culture and urban folk lifestyle of the city through his romantic involvement with the singer Soudamini, delving deeper and deeper into the mythologies of the local community in his endeavour to access the field of logic that he needed to draw upon to combat the arguments of his rival singer-debaters. Datta's full-throated singing and his capacity for larger than life performances built upon a realistic base, ably matched by the performances of professional veterans Jahar Ganguly (1903-69) and Ketaki Dutta (b. 1934), gave *Antony Kabiyal* a popularity that eluded most of the plays in the regular, professional theatre of the time. Datta's personal popularity, from *Antony Kabiyal*, and his 'softness' in handling his company leading to its slow disintegration, soon drove him out of theatre. The last years of his life Datta spent as a popular singer, singing traditional patriotic songs and theatre songs at concerts. Ketaki Dutta, his leading lady in *Antony Kabiyal*, has remained the only singer-actor after Datta to hold on to the rich Bengali tradition of the singing/singers' theatre.

Badal Sircar (b. 1925) made his dramatic shift from the proscenium theatre to the non-proscenium *angan-mancha* [lit. 'theatre in an intimate space'] in 1972. Till 1967, when he established the group Satabdi, Sircar, a professional architect, had been writing witty comedies, often takeoffs from Hollywood comedies, and staging a new one every year, usually for a single performance, with his group Chakra, an interesting group of economists, teachers, politically alert individuals from various walks of life, and their wives, most of them between their mid-thirties and mid-forties. Sircar and the group, an enlightened lot, took pride in the fact that they were amateurs, and their performances were marked by rich humour, exquisite taste and spontaneous naiveté. But a series of exposures between 1957 and 1967—to the works of Joan Littlewood, Yuri Lyubimov, the Cinoherni Klub Teater in Prague, and 'the last but not the least', Grotowski's *Apocalypsis cum Figuris* at Wroclaw, followed by a long interview with Grotowski—led Sircar to a more serious commitment to theatre, and the beginning of Satabdi. From 1968 to 1971 Satabdi performed fairly regularly a repertoire of comedies and a mixed bag of mood plays, plays of unregulated encounters, plays of ideas or plays that wove together episodes capturing the doubts and passions of a recent time span.

In 1970 Sircar was already a national figure, thanks to his play *Ebong Indrajit*. Written in 1963 as a 'private piece of writing' that he never thought of publishing or producing, it came to be published at a friend's insistence, and was lapped up by B.V. Karanth, Satyadev Dubey, Praveen Joshi, Shyamanand Jalan, Girish Karnad and Ammu Matthew, some of the country's best directors, who produced it in English, Hindi, Gujarati, and Kannada. But as a director, he maintained a low but distinctive profile, seeking to extend the sharp disruption he had brought to dramatic continuity in plays like *Ebong Indrajit* and *Baki Itihas* to his theatric practice; his intense involvement in the process leading him to abandon the picture frame stage forever and choose performance spaces recast and redesigned for specific plays, with the usual barriers/distances between performers and audience cancelled out to allow for immediate, direct communication.

From *Ballabhpurer Rupkatha* (1970), a comedy about a genial, aristocratic, romantically inclined ghost with the looks of his living descendant, who creates a riot of confusion, Sircar moved to a theatre of concern and conscience. He began addressing issues like the rural-urban divide, with the metropolis claiming all the available resources and facilities, pauperizing the village in the process (*Bhoma*, 1976); slavery and revolt in history, drawing on the revolt of Spartacus in Italy (*Spartacus*, 1973) and a tribal revolt in Bengal in 1855 (*Basi Khabar*, 1979); aspects of capitalism and visions of emancipation from capitalism (*Prastab*, 1973; *Bhanga Manush*, 1976; *Hattamalar Oparey*, 1977; *Bhul Rasta*, 1989); violence, particularly state violence and war (*Tringsha Shatabdi*, 1974, a documentary play on Hiroshima and Nagasaki; *Khat-Mat-Kring*, 1983).

For nearly three decades now Sircar has stayed resolutely away from the proscenium theatre, and from marketing his theatre. His choice of undefined performance spaces, in small halls without a raised platform, public parks, open spaces virtually anywhere, college and university campuses, anti-nuke demonstrations, and his firm resolve never to advertise in the media or charge for admission form part of an anti-capitalist project. For a time, he described his theatre as 'the third theatre' (the other two being the traditional village theatre and the city theatre, with 'its roots in the Western soil') as 'an attempt to create a Theatre of Synthesis', analysing 'both the theatre forms to find the exact points of strength and weakness and their causes' for clues to the synthesis. But as it developed an ideology of its own, he came to call it 'free theatre', free from constraints imposed by a capitalist power structure, and offered free of cost to the people. Sircar has opted out of the mainstream theatre of experimental groups, and lives a marginal existence, with a bunch of small groups sharing his philosophy and commitment and performing regularly to small audiences within the city and in villages and small towns.

Committed to a long term engagement with his audience, Sircar has adapted—to the needs and perceptions of his wideflung audience—several modern classics like *The Caucasian Chalk Circle* (1978), *Marat/Sade* (1980), *Woza Albert* (1987), and *Androcles and the Lion* (1991)—and major modern novels in Bengali like *Naginikanyar Kahini* by Tarashankar Bandyopadhyay in 1982, and *Padmanadir Majhi* by Manik Bandyopadhyay in 1990. In his *Androcles and the Lion*, Sircar gives his emancipatory politics an ecstatic comic flourish with Androcles and the lion dancing out of the stage in a bonding that extends humanity beyond its conventional confines.

At the other extreme from Sircar, was Tarun Roy (1927-88). Marginalized from the strongly Left-oriented non-professional theatre in Calcutta, thanks to his association with the ruling Congress and its politics, he retained, through the sixties, in a small hundred-seater theatre in his own house, a kind of continuity with the acting style of the late Sisirkumar Bhaduri. Bhaduri had, in the twenties and the thirties, brought to the more conventional Bengali style of acting (larger-than-life and strongly sentimental) a psychologically credible, rounded and consistent realism. Even while continuing his explorations in the Bhaduri style, which still had enough riches to deliver, in the early seventies, in two consecutive productions (*Parajita Nayak*, 1980; and *Athacha Sanjukta*, 1972), Roy and his group, Theatre Centre, offered an agonized view of an older generation confronting the moral waste that it has made of its life, and looking with precarious and doubting hope to a rebellious younger generation committed to violence.

The new directors that came into their own in the seventies were Bibhash Chakraborty (b. 1937), Arun Mukherjee (b. 1937), Manoj Mitra (b. 1938), Soumitra Chatterjee (b. 1935), Kumar Roy (b. 1926), Rudraprasad Sengupta (b. 1935), Jochhan Dastidar (1931-98), Nilkantha Sengupta (b. 1946) and Dwijen Banerjee (b. 1949).

Both Chakraborty and Sengupta had begun their careers in Nandikar, with Ajitesh Bandyopadhyay as their mentor. In 1966, Chakraborty led a split from Nandikar, to form Theatre Workshop. In two consecutive productions, *Rajrakta* (1971) and *Chakbhanga Madhu* (1972), Chakraborty established himself as a major director. Mohit Chattopadhyay (b. 1934) and Manoj Mitra, the respective playwrights, represented two different genres altogether—the former, a master in using language to throw up powerful images of power and its machinations, allowing theatre to build up on these images in acting style, tonal variations, variations in pace in both speech and action, and in stage design with non-real objects; the latter, more grounded in earthy reality with flights of whimsy highlighting emotional attachments and obsessions that disrupt the norms of objective reality and illuminate spaces of more humane subjectivity.

It was Shyamal Ghosh (b. 1933), in the sixties who had, in Chattopadhyay's *Mrityu Sangbad* (1965) and *Chandralokey Agnikanda* (1967), discovered the features of a strikingly original poetic drama in prose, for which he designed a theatric style in which levels and modes of acting clashed with or evoked levels of emotional existence, with the outsider challenging, questioning and subverting the mores of everyday domesticity.

Mohit Chattopadhyay's profound discontent with the spirit of abject acquiescence that rules middle-class existence acquired a strong political character in *Rajrakta*, where he virtually charges the middle class with nurturing, supporting and sustaining an everyday fascism. Chattopadhyay's suggestion of the different faces of authority demanded a continuity of translations between the different impersonations of authority. Director Chakraborty allowed a repeated question-and-answer pattern ('What are they throwing?'—'They are throwing stones') to glide tonally from a schoolmaster-in-the classroom situation to a sentry, who in his turn ever so casually wraps a shawl around himself, puts on spectacles, and starts snoring, to become a father. A young man and a young woman cajoled, threatened and intimidated in turns by Authority, in the form of a Rajasahib, fight for survival and freedom at the core of the play. While the transitions and appearances varied, the appearances going into wild caricature, conventional stage types and expressionist idealizations or distortions, the setting had a quality of cold hardness and the trope—'Keep everything in place, don't remove anything'—repeated with tonal variations, remained the voice of Authority maintaining the status quo. Chakraborty handled the confrontations between authority and youth episodically, allowing each episode an autonomy, never repeating a pattern.

If *Rajrakta* was a masterpiece of conscious style, *Chakbhanga Madhu*, in Chakraborty's Theatre Workshop production, was a rugged, realistic narrative of exploitation and the violence in opposition that it draws forth, with the characters often manifesting the elemental desires and passions born of the survival instinct with literally stunning force.

In a wide range of productions, including adaptations of Brecht's *Lux in tenebris* and *Schweik*, Dario Fo's *Accidental Death* and *Trumpets and Raspberries*, and plays by Tagore and Mohit Chattopadhyay and Manoj Mitra, Chakraborty has shown signs of a director's sensitivity to different dramatic idioms. His *Madhab Malanchi Kainya* (1988), a folk ballad, made into a colourful, slick, musical production, for his new group, Anya Theatre, founded in 1985, proved to be a significant departure from his more politically oriented works, and a popular hit.

Chetana, founded in 1972 by actor-director Arun Mukherjee, came to notice with its productions of *Mareech Sangbad* (1973) and *Jagannath* (1977); the former dovetailing and flitting to and fro, through musical transitions—satiric-balladic choruses led by singer-actor Biplabketan Chakrabarty—between three parallel narratives of individuals struggling under political pressure—in a Ramayana story, in the United States during the Vietnam War, and in a Bengal village; the latter used a freewheeling mix of flashback, memory and emotionally charged fragments to tell the story (modelled on Lu Xun's *Ah Q*) of a man who becomes a martyr and hero in spite of himself. Mukherjee's own performance as a weak and wavering man drifting with circumstances till he finds and cherishes an identity not of his own free choice, created a fresh modern stereotype that came to be picked up later in both theatre and cinema.

In 1977, playwright Manoj Mitra turned director with his *Sajano Bagan* for the group Sundaram (founded in 1957, but for all practical purposes resuscitated by Mitra in 1977). *Sajano Bagan* is still a popular item in the repertoire, twenty years later. The strength of *Sajano Bagan* and Mitra's subsequent productions of his own plays lies in the originality of his texts and his own performances as actor, marked by his capacity for and mastery of intense physicality manifest in delicate, controlled movements of the limbs and shifts and changes in facial expression, employed to lift his 'real' characters to the level of the unreal. The performance, accomplished in realistic detail, itself achieves the flight from reality—evident at its striking best in the old man in *Sajano Bagan*, who, decrepit to the point of having lost the use of his legs and floundering on to the stage on his haunches at the beginning of the play, signs away his orchard to the neighbouring landowner on condition that he will be fed and clothed and sustained by the latter till he dies. Then the orchard would become the landowner's for ever. But even as the greedy landowner waits for the old man to die, a distantly related young couple put him back on his legs, in a desperate bid for the security of a home for themselves and their expected child; the old man's return to life blends magic and the elemental urge to survive.

Brecht had made his entry into the Bengali theatre scene with *Galileo*, in a translation by Ritwik Ghatak, better known as a film-maker, in a production by the teaching faculty of Burdwan University, in December 1964. The seventies had seen several Brecht adaptations in Bengali, with three versions of *The Good Person of Szechwan* running simultaneously in 1974. But it was left to Sekhar Chatterjee (1924-90) to discover 'the real Brecht at last' (as a review recognized), with his *Pontu Laha* (1975), from Brecht's *Herr Puntila and His Man Matti*. He captured the basic simplicity of the scheme, which stands dangerously close to the simplistic and the crude, needing art to recognize its quality, and restraint to make poetry of the vulgar: a couple of drunks, master and retainer, squatting down to urinate before a lamppost, or the fat ugly man having a bath. Chatterjee treated all these with rare balance and a sense of innocent humour, never overplaying drunkenness, for here it is more a state of the mind than a state of the nerves. Arany Banerjee's stage design, with walking papiermache trees, lampposts and houses, had a carnival or folkplay freedom; space and distance lending beauty to the settings, a tinsel moon or a car stalled against a toppled lamppost becoming poetry.

Variations on realism have marked the works of the other directors who emerged in the seventies, in the tempestuous political scenario of West Bengal which allowed for a vibrant theatre, critical, cynical, and passionate by turns. This period saw a truncated Left seeking to snatch power from the Congress (the party in power), in a desperate battle which it ultimately wins, but not before repressing with cynical brutality the more radical opposition within the Left, and surviving an Emergency which it turned to good account.

The sheer range and criticality of the seventies sadly pales in the eighties and nineties, with a Left Front, firmly saddled in power in the state, taking the wind out of the sails of an oppositionist theatre. Older directors who have made their presence felt in the last two decades include Kumar Roy, who came to lead and direct Bohurupee after the exit of the Mitras, and showed a fine literary taste—not always theatrically translated in its entirety—for Sanskrit classics, plays by Tagore, Brecht and Sartre, and a new playwright, Sisirkumar Das. Das has a penchant for devices like the double, or the dead man come alive to confront his surviving contemporaries, with the critical function of questioning a fall from earlier values. Soumitra Chatterjee, an outstanding actor on stage and screen, adapted plays like *The Big Knife, The Matchmaker, Sleuth* and *Lifeline*, as vehicles for virtuoso performances, with a fine sense of theatric space. And Asit Mukherjee (b. 1936) , first with Gandhar, and now, more recently, with Chupkatha, offered adaptations of Miller's *The Price*, Arbuzov's *Old Times*, and Gibson's *The Miracle Worker*, graduating from low key interactions between a small set of characters in a limited space to the high drama of a mute child 'finding' her voice.

Rudraprasad Sengupta (b. 1935) and Ashok Mukherjee (b. 1940) have kept their groups Nandikar and Theatre Workshop running at a level of competence, with their directorial achievements never quite touching the heights of their predecessors. However, both at Chetana and Nandikar, a new generation of young directors have emerged in the nineties—Suman Mukherjee at Chetana, with *Gantabya* (1997), on Dr Norman Bethune in Spain and China; and Gautam Haldar at Nandikar, with his *Meghnadbadh Kabya* (1995), a one-man rendition of a nineteenth-century secondary epic, exhibiting a flair for music, rhythm, and choreography, with excellent live musical support on stage from Swatilekha Sengupta, who came up later with her own one-woman piece, *Shanu Raychaudhury* (1998).

Kaushik Sen is yet another actor-director who came into his

own with a brilliant production of *Pratham Partha*, a poetic drama by Buddhadev Bose, one of the major modern poets of the language, taking a fresh look at some of the hidden histories of characters in the Mahabharata; poetry and sound and choreography giving the work a distance that is dynamic and metamorphic.

In fact, the most significant feature of theatre in Calcutta in the eighties and nineties has been the emergence of a band of women directors—Usha Ganguli (b. 1945) and her Rangakarmee, with *Court Martial* (1991), *Rudali* (1992), *Himmatmai* (1998); Sohag Sen (b. 1946) and her Ensemble, with *Uttaradhikar* (1989) and *Party* (1990), both by the Marathi playwright Mahesh Elkunchwar, and *Mahanirvan* (1993) by yet another Marathi playwright, Satish Alekar; Jayoti Bose (b. 1953) and Sutrapat, with *Care Kori Na* (1993) and *Robot Kupokat* (1994); and Ishita Mukhopadhyay (b.1963) and Ushnik, with *Kamalkamini* (1993).

The women directors have all carved their distinctive niches in the theatre scene. Usha Ganguli, performing in Hindi in a primarily Bengali speaking region, is perhaps offering the largest number of shows of the largest live repertoire of any Calcutta group. Sohag Sen has introduced major contemporary Indian playwrights writing in other languages to the Bengali-speaking audience, underscoring social processes of change which operate in the same manner throughout the country. Jayoti Bose and her company of adult actors playing teenagers for a teenager audience, Grips Theatre style, have opened up a new area of social interaction through theatre. Ishita Mukhopadhyay's *Kamalkamini*, featuring Ketaki Dutta, a singer-actress, with a long professional track record, reconstructed in theatric terms a social history of the actress in Bengal.

Calcutta has had its share of visiting directors—Hansguenther Heyme and Fritz Bennewitz—producing *Antigone* and *Galileo* and *King Lear* with local actors—adding more colour to the scene than authentic theatric values.

The stills gathered in this volume will evoke a lot of memories, and may serve as sources of inspiration for a theatre going through a patchy and dull phase at the close of the nineties.

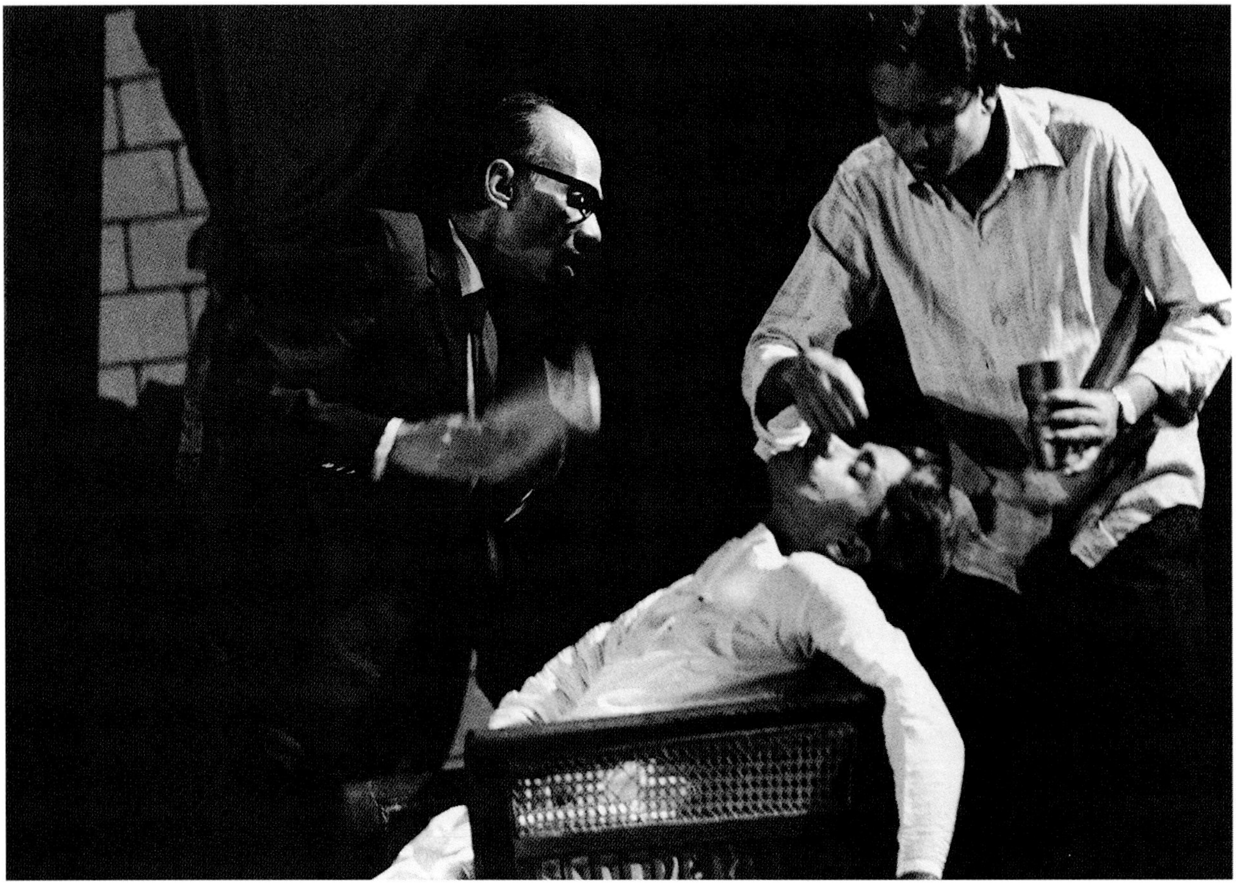

Ballabhpurer Rupkatha

We talk and write about the beauty of art, the sacredness of art, the human need for art, yet we can think of no way of dealing with art except as a commodity, to be bought and sold in the market, like food, clothes, shelter, education and all other necessities of life. We do not even consider that to be a contradiction.

We have more or less taken it for granted that we cannot resolve any of these contradictions. We have learnt to live with them. So much so, that if we see anybody trying to make a beginning in the attempt to resolve any one of the contradictions, we consider that person mad. That consideration does not always remain passive, particularly if the mad person's activity makes us feel guilty in any way. Then we come up with condemnation and slander, persecution and ostracization, even with violence.

. . . in the early seventies, a handful of people embarked on a voyage that led to the resolution of at least one contradiction in the chaotic scenario, thus definitively enlisting themselves in the small band of mad people. In a system in which all the basic necessities of life can be obtained only at a price, they tried to find out if at least one art medium as important as the theatre could be made free for all people. I happened to be one of them, and I still am.

But is that all? Was that how that voyage began—aiming at the port of 'free theatre' with a well-delineated map in hand? No, it was not like that. There were other voyages before that voyage. Not just false starts, but voyages important to our theatre, important to our life. Theatre and life—are they separable? They were, in the beginning; but what about later? What about now?

. . . Same as others of our class and kind, we did not even believe that a free theatre was possible. We had accepted the city theatre—the proscenium stage and the auditorium, the sets and the spotlights, in short the theatre imported from Britain more than a century back, and thereby we had accepted the fact that theatre cost money. But we were frantically trying to reduce the cost of production. We made a principle of not spending more than a hundred rupees for a new production on sets, props and costumes taken together. We recycled the set elements made for one production by making platform modules. We met the challenge by spending only sixty-five rupees in creating the set for *Ballabhpurer Rupkatha*—three fluted columns and a throne in the court room of a dilapidated palace. *Abu Hossein* demanded sets for court room and garden, parlour and street, and we needed less than a hundred rupees for all that. We learnt to use our imagination and the imagination of the audience. But we did all this not with the thought of a free theatre, but in order to survive as a theatre group.

[. . .] I must also mention another landmark in our voyages. That was in July, 1974, before the state of Emergency. The authorities were trying in various ways to stop the Saturday performances at Surendranath Park, without much success. Ultimately, in a brutal attack by the police one Saturday afternoon, an innocent young spectator called Prabir Dutta was killed. Moreover, some members of the theatre group which was to perform on that day (it happened to be the group that initiated the Saturday performances at that park) were arrested. They were identified by police informers even when they were in the bus terminus, quite a way from the park. However, there was a massive protest on the part of the Calcutta citizens, as well as the artistes. I doubt very much whether such a massive protest will ever occur again in Calcutta for a similar occasion. On one Saturday five weeks after the incident, the right to perform at Surendranath Park was re-established by a rally of ten thousand, in which almost all the personalities in the fields of theatre and films participated. Apart from addresses, recitation of poems, and songs, a symbolic performance of *Michhil* was presented, in which representatives of various theatre groups participated.

But at the end of the programme people were asking us, that is to say those who have been performing in that park, whether the Saturday shows would continue henceforth or not. We could not assure them, rather we said that it was not likely, for we did not know what would happen when the protection of numbers and names would be missing. Later on we discussed amongst ourselves and ventured on the performance next Saturday. We laid out a detailed plan, and when, according to the plan, we entered the park simultaneously in bands of twos and threes from different sides of the park, we were greatly astonished to find a gathering of about three thousand people patiently waiting for us, although we had told them that there was hardly any likelihood of our coming to perform. From then on, the Saturday performances continued till the promulgation of the state of Emergency, and they began again on the Saturday after the Emergency was withdrawn.

Badal Sircar

Androcles O Singha

শতাব্দী
অঙ্গনমঞ্চ

Hattamalar Oparey

The Night Is Green

. . . Now is the time
To believe in past lies,
Now is the time to conjure up
Lies for the future,
Now is the time to be dead
In momentary dreams—
Green in wishful lies
And senile content

Badal Sircar
25 August 1958.

Banglar Mati

The curtain came down at the first interval in *Banglar Mati* on the Bengali Hindu heroine going away with her next door neighbour, a young Muslim man, to Calcutta. The audience, made up mostly of refugees from East Pakistan, broke into a furore: 'Do you expect us to accept a Hindu girl going away with a Muslim man, one of those who persecuted us and drove us away from our homes? Stop the play at once.' They began pelting stones at the stage.

Tulsi Lahiri, the playwright, came out, stood before the curtain and addressed the audience: 'You have to listen to me. Only then will I listen to you. Like many of you, I too was driven out of East Bengal. I don't know what you left behind. Do you know what I left behind? I had worked hard for years to raise the money to buy books to set up a rich library. All my life's earnings went into that enormous library. They have now taken away that library of mine, leaving me a pauper. And with all that behind me, I have written this play. A playwright has his religion to live by. The spectators too have a religion. It is part of the playwright's religion to close the play with a suggestion, or in plays of a certain kind, to leave something to the audience, something that they will brood on. The audience must wait for that conclusion. What right have you to stop the play when it is only half way through? Do you have any clue as to how the play will end? I challenge you—if you cannot tell me how it ends, I'll let you lay down the punishment that you'll take from me. You owe it to the playwright to watch the play till the end. If at the end of it you still find it objectionable, you are free to put a garland of shoes around my neck. But you must have the patience to watch it till the end.'

The rest of the peformance carried on unhindered. At the end of it, Lahiri was loaded with garlands of flowers.

Sabitabrata Datta

Kolkatar Hamlet

I was provoked by the cowardice of a theatre—inheritors of a tradition that had once shaken up the colonial rulers—that did not have the guts in the late sixties or the early seventies to take stock of a political situation in which young men were being gunned down in the streets of Calcutta, or even give an insertion in the Press condoling the death of Satyen Mitra, a playwright-actor, shot to death. And then, when the police broke up a crowd gathered at Curzon Park to watch a street play, and killed Prabir Dutta, and I went out to mobilize a protest, there was the distinguished actor-director who refused to be a party to it because he preferred to trust the official police version disclaiming responsibility. I was not expecting anyone to attack a police outpost to register protest. But when people in theatre do not shed a tear for a colleague killed, I do not find any sense in their doing theatre. The theatre is for humanity. If it abandons humanity, and turns into a free-for-all for pimps and suckers, then it is better to give up theatre altogether. It was Satyen-da's killing that was the immediate provocation for my *Kolkatar Hamlet* [Calcutta's Hamlet (1973)]. I conceived a situation where someone I had met and talked to, the evening before, is killed at midnight, and when I discover and stand before the dead body the following morning, Satyen-da stands up and challenges me, 'So nobody did a thing, nobody said a word!' The silence was a symptom of a degeneration, a test case that demonstrated how a half-educated middle class had brought the dream of a people's theatre down to the level of a theatre for personal gain.

Asit Bose

Bidehi

Dansagar

Pontu Laha

My first attempt at Brecht was *Arturo Ui*. The reason for choosing this play was the political atmosphere in our country at that time. It was 1972. This being a historical play, and my first venture, I depended on the model given in the *Theaterarbeit*. The details of the costumes and even the sets were more or less on the same lines. The play was well taken in Calcutta. The audience encouraged me and insisted that I should take it to the people. I did, and I flopped. I was disappointed. But I sat back and reasoned. I discovered that the Second World War was a distant reality to our people. They have hardly ever experienced the real impact of any war as yet. The ignorant village people might have felt it in their stomach as inflation and scarcity of food. But that is always there. They might have heard the name of Hitler but they knew nothing

Pontu Laha

about the concentration camps or what fascism really is. And on top of everything else, the capitalistic system, which ultimately leads to fascism, is not known to them. What should I do, then? Who is to educate them? I faced many questions. I dropped it because, I thought, it was no use doing it for the city elites, who are aware of these facts anyway, but will do nothing. At best they will praise my play, discuss the aesthetics, discuss alienation and snore at home.

I still believed I have to take Brecht to the people. They are the people Brecht was concerned about—the exploited and ignorant masses who did not know that the miseries they lived in were man-made, and that this state can be changed.

My second attempt was *Puntila* [*Pontu Laha*]. With this

I thought I could communicate with the rural audience who are still living under a feudal land set-up. But how about the class conflict? Will they be able to understand this? Never mind, I said, the play is simple and has so many things common to their experience. At least they know their masters, and they know that they are their servants. It is an everyday reality in their lives.

I want to make the production as simple and comprehensive as possible, keeping, of course, the Brechtian dialectics in mind. I attempted a device to keep the class element always in focus. I put two stickers under the jackets of Puntila and Matti, one reading 'The Master', the other reading 'The Servant'—just to hammer in on the audience the social relationship between the two—throughout the performance. When Puntila insists and Matti willy-nilly concedes that they are equal, and they stand side by side measuring against each other, and they take an oath that they are equals, the stickers still show under their jackets.

As a device to explain to the audience that Puntila's drunkenness was not a state of the nerves, but one of the mind, I made Puntila wear a cap, a cap of the kind used by the leaders of our ruling party, but the colour was different. It was saffron, symbolizing religion. Thus I combined politics with religion. And to establish this, I used a ritual. When, in the pub scene, Puntila discovers a human being in Matti and offers him a drink—they hold the glasses up and freeze—in comes a girl—dancing to music with a silver plate on her head and the saffron cap on it. She stops and Matti steps out dancing, picks it up and puts it on Puntila's head. The dancing girl disappears—Puntila livens up, and he is a transformed man. From now on, whenever he is drunk Matti puts the cap on his head, and whenever he is sober, Puntila flings it away. The device worked.

Sekhar Chatterjee

Chhayanot

Jagannath

I came into theatre as an actor, acting those bits one does in school and college theatricals. There was no clear comprehension then of a dramatic sense or the role and function of theatre, or its social relevance. But all those notions came in fast enough. Early in my acting career I realized that I would not go far with acting. My voice had congenital limitations. Once I realized that, early enough in my life, I knew that I could be more effective as a director, for by then I had fallen in love with theatre. My initial interest in theatre grew from various factors—the praise I got for my performance, and other things—but there were several stages before I came to serious theatre. I came to the group theatre movements much later, when I formed Chetana in 1972.

Even in Chetana, I came to acting only in *Jagannath* (1977), when the group was already four or five years old. . . Ten years of deliberation had gone into the making of *Jagannath*. I am not a playwright. I couldn't ever have conceived a character like Jagannath. I was responding to Lu Xun, and building on him. But there was great satisfaction when I could ultimately bring the experience to an Indian context, relate it to Indian politics, and make a credible character out of Jagannath, drawing on whatever little I knew of the lower middle class in India. But viewers had their personal perceptions of Jagannath. One of the critics commented: 'Jagannath doesn't understand a thing.' There are such critics. Several leftwing intellectuals misread the scene of sex and hunger. They said that this was physically impossible. The woman is aware that this is a hungry man. She is a victim of sexual oppression. Her husband has thrown her out. The woman finds him safe. With him it will not blow up into a scandal. Nobody would come to know of it. That is why she has chosen to approach Jagannath. But she has brought food for him, too. She has to feed the man first, to arouse his sexual instinct. The question of sex and hunger is linked to that of possession.

Why and how is one possessed? How does a possessed woman act? I have seen people in fits of possession. I have a sort of obsession with several religious phenomena. In the house in which I grew up, where I spent my childhood, there used to be all kinds of religious rituals, with gurus and their tricks. I saw them all. Several of these experiences have made their way into *Jagannath* and given it its reality.

Arun Mukherjee

Antigone

Rajrakta

The prevailing political environment was charged with passion, commitment, and an ideology. Maybe it lacked a scientific approach, and was more dream and passion—not strong in a discipline of thought. The passion centred on a leftwing vision of the future of the country, seeking to figure out how the people of the country would struggle for their rights and achieve their real freedom—and these political thoughts came to be reflected in the plays.

I was fascinated by Mohit's [Mohit Chattopadhyay, playwright] fun, grotesquerie, his weird constructions of dialogue. His extraordinary wit and humour held a tremendous appeal for me. In his personal conversation, as well as in his dramatic dialogues, his use of and play with words was so remarkable that I once described him as a real *kathashilpi* [i.e. an artist of words]. When I read his *Guineapig* renamed *Rajrakta*, I instinctively felt—this was my material. For in *Guineapig*, I found the political dimension that was missing in his earlier plays. What delighted me even more was the discovery that here was a political play that was entirely different from the conventional pattern of political plays, and yet was so intensely political. I found it a deadly weapon.

Bibhash Chakraborty

Chakbhanga Madhu

Chakbhanga Madhu

Of all the productions of my plays directed by others, the one that pleased me most, in fact thrilled me, was *Chakbhanga Madhu* [Hive-fresh Honey (1972)], directed by Bibhash Chakraborty for Theatre Workshop. I enjoyed working with them. I would call it 'work', for I did a lot of work with them besides writing—all that with a lot of excitement. Bibhash himself had directed barely a couple or so of plays by then. He was bubbling with energy and so full of ideas.

I have noticed in most cases that the points of strength in my plays, the points I drive at, whether in situation or in dialogue, get lost, with the emphasis coming somewhere else, to the point of contradicting it. This would be as true for an insignificant playwright like me as for a master. The director must have the sensitivity to tap that delicate, concealed point in the play . . .

It did not happen with *Chakbhanga Madhu*, because Bibhash could identify with the milieu. Bibhash made me give several readings of the play. At an earlier stage I had thought of producing it for my theatre group. Then Soumitra Chatterjee, the well known stage and screen actor, had thought of producing it. In the process I had read the play at least fifty times. I would read it again and again and make corrections every day. I had to read it out so many times that I reached a point when I could act out all the roles with my voice conveying what each of them wore, where they were dozing, where they rose to their feet, what parts of the dialogue they spoke sleepily—I could convey all that in my voice, like an elaborate scenario. So Bibhash made a cassette of my reading, and listened to it for days to acquire the dialect. Still unsatisfied, he wanted to go to the village, to the interior. So we made a trip to the village, to the interior, where we collected folk ballads and songs. That was a production that tapped every point of the text to perfection.

Manoj Mitra

Narak Guljar

Having watched my Schweik, in 1981, a friend said, 'You've acted in the style of Chaplin.' He was obviously paying me a compliment, but it came as a shock to me . . . The individual style that Chaplin had developed through meticulous observation and a rich perfectionism remains inimitable. It would be foolish to try to emulate him . . . Moreover, there is a fundamental difference between Schweik and Chaplin. The characters played by Chaplin are not verbally inclined, while Schweik is all speech—crammed with words. Schweik creates with his words a spell of bewilderment. Yet how can people see anything in common between the two? Perhaps because they share a common point of view, a common philosophy. They find the contradictions, the lies masquerading as justice, and impotence in the name of objectivity, rampant in society, as objects of ridicule that they would undauntedly kick around with deadly satire. Brecht had perhaps—why perhaps, most certainly—been charmed by the spontaneous impudence of Chaplin's little man, the tramp, and given him yet another identity.

Bibhash Chakraborty

Schweik Gelo Juddhey

Madhab Malanchi Kainya

For twenty-five long years in theatre I have sought diversity. I had begun at the extremist pole of naturalism, with Sartre's *The Respectable Prostitute* and Sean O' Casey's *Juno and the Paycock*, only to realize that it was almost impossible to reach or cross the level that my more successful elders, Sombhu Mitra, Utpal Dutt and Ajitesh Bandyopadhyay, had achieved with their productions of Ibsen, Gorky and Chekhov a little while before my appearance in Bengali theatre. A passion for adventure soon drove me to coasts where these men had never geared their vessels. In this quest of mine I have endeavoured to rediscover contemporary playwrights, like Mohit Chattopadhyay . . . and Manoj Mitra . . . At the same time I have dared to tackle the works of some of the most celebrated playwrights of our country and abroad. This other list has included Brecht and Rabindranath Tagore on one hand, and Dario Fo and Utpal Dutt on the other.

More recently I had the feeling that Bengali theatre had somehow lost the courage and daring to experiment with themes and theatric styles. Everybody seemed to have decided to play safe and chosen to tread the paths much trodden by our masters. Attempts were being made occasionally to set up this lack of courage as a matter of principle or as a chosen ideal. It was a mode of thinking that had virtually banished the elements of folk culture from modern theatre. It was a tendency that could be described, in theatre, at least, as a kind of Western purism or fundamentalism. At the same time, Bengali audiences responded warmly and enthusiastically to theatre from other states. They were already complaining that Bengali theatre workers were cut off from the folk life and culture of the region, and they were turning away from the monotony of the theatre.

Thus the idea of *Madhab Malanchi Kainya* came from a commitment to theatre. There was no noble zeal to revive a folk culture dead in the process of time, there was no running after the 'ethnic' or 'folk' fad; there was only the desire to enrich our theatre with this experiment in a new style, there was an urge to draw the contemporary audience into the orbit of new theatric experience. *Madhab Malanchi Kainya* dramatizes a simple narrative from the ancient Mymensingh Geetika of eastern Bengal. The Geetika is a narrative form, no doubt, but it is no folk drama. We have attempted to confront and recast the original form, character and narrative of the Geetika, and presented it in terms of modern theatre practice.

I was drawn to the narrative primarily on two counts. Firstly, I admired the valour and unconventionality of an ordinary Bengali woman from three hundred years ago, qualities still quite rare. Secondly, I was overwhelmed by its vision of life, a sense of close community unaffected by discriminations of religion, caste or status, something that must have been real some day and is only a dream and a yearning today, cherished by men of goodwill.

Bibhash Chakraborty

Sombhu Mitra left Bohurupee in 1978. The last new production he directed was in 1971. From 1971 to 1978 he acted regularly in the ongoing productions of Bohurupee, but declared that he wouldn't take up any new plays. The void that was gradually taking shape, now stared us rudely in the face when he left in 1978. It was a very critical phase. By all parameters of logic, an organization isn't supposed to exist in a situation where such a void has been created. But the group could withstand the crisis, perhaps because of the kind of discipline that had been instilled into it.

In the midst of this vacuum, we decided to do *Mrichhakatik*. I still consider myself fortunate because I had the courage to take such a decision. This has a kind of historic importance because this play was unlike plays we were used to doing. Bohurupee didn't have a tradition of doing Sanskrit plays; we didn't have a model before us, and we had the freedom. It was also a kind of a challenge, because I wanted the audience to be perfectly at ease with the play. So it was up to us what we would take from the Natyashastra and how we would blend it with the infrastructure available to us in the proscenium. [. . .] another important exercise while putting up the play was planning the costumes, and here I am indebted to Khaled Chowdhury, because he showed me the way. He had designed some unique costumes for an earlier Bohurupee production *Swargiya Prahasan* [premiered on 22 May 1955 in New Empire, Calcutta]. The costumes were made of jute, with only two or three natural earth colours being used as colouring agents. That lent a kind of antiquity to the costumes. I consider myself fortunate because I was able to watch Khaled-da while he was working—on sets or even while drawing or designing. We got Suren Chakrabarty to do the costumes for us. We used canvas instead of jute and used the ancient sculptures as models while designing the costumes—the *nibibandha* [a wide decorative belt for the waist used by women], the folds adorning the front of the lower garment, the *uttariya* [a loose drape for the torso]. We used as models for the *pagdi* [head-dress], real *pagdis* from the museum at Amarkantak.

Kumar Roy

Mrichhakatik

To me, the charm of a character lies in the shades and nuances present in it. This I found in full measure in Brecht's play *Galileo.* The play orchestrates to a crescendo in the last scene of the play when Galileo speaks about the role of science. This should be spoken with absolute detachment, shorn of all emotion, and here lies the Brechtian touch—we see a great scientist speaking, and yet we are also made aware that he is human and has common human frailties. I feel that the most moving portion of the play is where Galileo, who has a feeling of guilt gnawing at him all the time, confesses: Yes, I know I have done wrong. I have said things that are scientifically incorrect; but I was afraid. I was terrified of physical torture. I tried to work on his feeling of guilt throughout the play and bring it out very, very subtly in the portrayal of the character of Galileo.

Kumar Roy

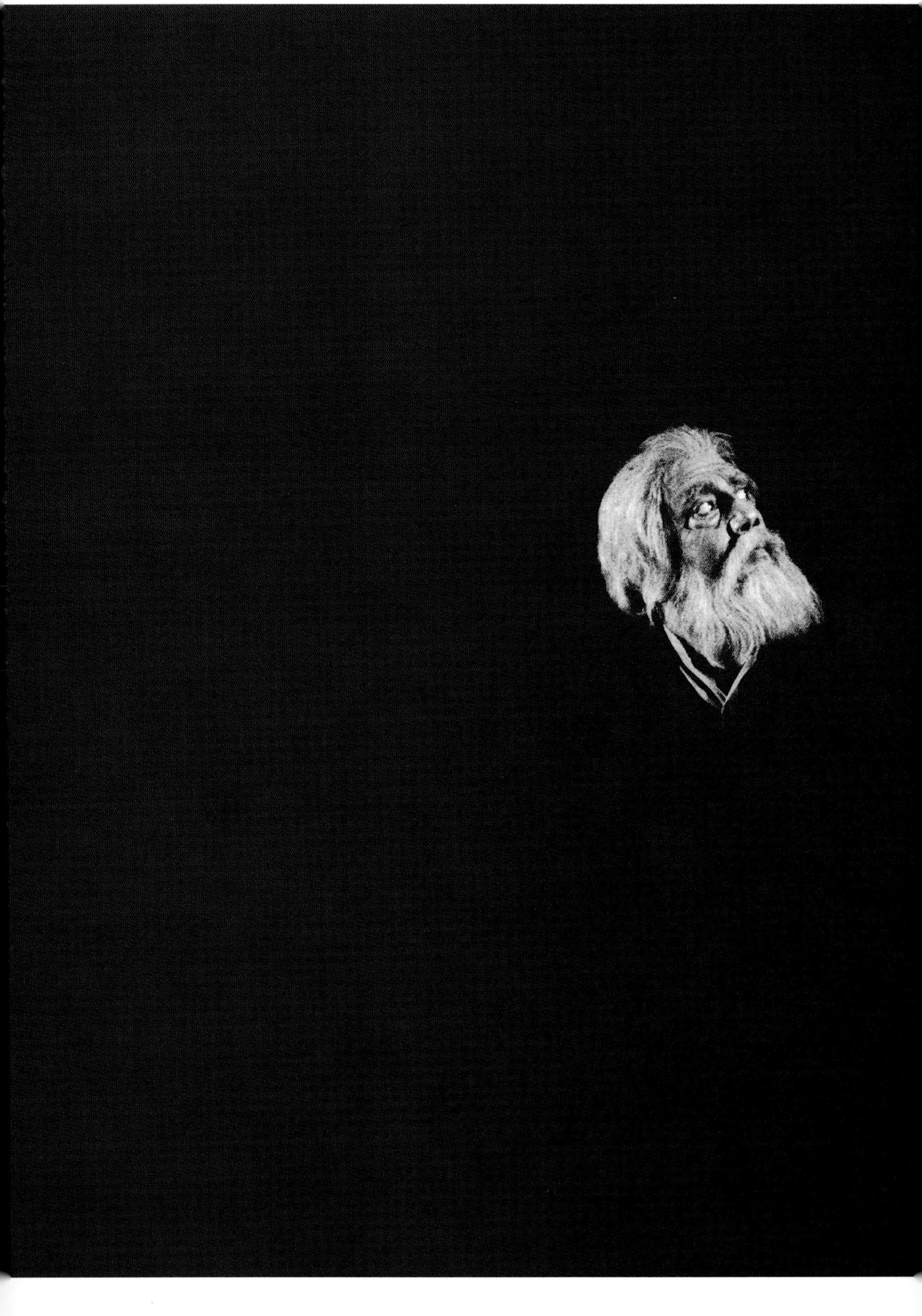

Galileo

Nindapankey

Sartre had employed a unique critique of history and politics in this play—something I found extremely relevant to our times. I felt we needed a pragmatic view at that point of time because it was a time when political machinations and opportunism had crossed the limits of decency. The situation isn't any better today, but that is how I felt. I thought the play would have done a lot of good to our misdirected policies. But people here started a false propaganda saying it was anti-communist. It was a good production. . . given the chance, I'll do this play again. This is right time to do it.

Kumar Roy

Akbar-Birbal

The Babri Masjid incident took place just before we decided to do the play and each of us tried to protest in our own way. So when Sisir Das gave us this play, we found that there was nothing overly direct, at the same time the rudiments have been questioned, the genesis of the conflict has been traced to the very roots of Indian history . . . and the realization that had religion been based on humanism (something that Akbar and Birbal had tried to create), it wouldn't have taken such a turn. There was this little girl from Afghanistan in the play, who tries her best to be friends with everybody, but is confronted with a situation she finds utterly confusing. It was a soft, mellow note in the play.

Kumar Roy

In the first draft that Manoj [Mitra] had given us, the court scene was missing. Just imagine what the play would have been without that crucial scene! This was sometime in 1980/81 when the entire country was taken up by a great 'folk' revival. For *Rajdarshan* we planned to bring in certain folk elements and adapt them to the requirements of the proscenium . . . The other thing I found interesting in the play was how two people—a social parasite who lives off others, and a blacksmith who has to work hard to earn his living—respond to the same situation. Both have gone to seek *darshan* [audience] with the king. Just consider the fun and the irony of it all—going for a *rajdarshan*, the blacksmith realizes where the *darshan* [philosophy] of the king has gone wrong, and the parasite accepts this flawed philosophy unquestioningly. I took care not to typecast the character of the blacksmith into the typical 'trade union' mould. He is just a very ordinary man who has to earn his bread by the sweat of his brow. He operates by sheer common sense. It is something that comes almost instinctively to him. Once he realizes what is wrong he wants to come back to his village, to his roots, with all his heart and soul. For me the play is about a return, a going back to one's roots.

Kumar Roy

Rajdarshan

Sankhapurer Sukanya

Bertolt Brecht's *The Good Person of Szechwan* has been a favourite of Indian directors. Nandikar once did a production of this play which was quite popular. So why produce the same old play in a fresh new adaptation all over again? I could spin off scores of reasons—that it is always beneficial to do the classics over and over again, that this play allows you to involve several actors and offers the space for an interplay of ideas, or even that it is a way of atoning for the Nandikar production of 1974 (which was a 'hit' no doubt, but for all the wrong reasons), or simply that I love this play.

But I feel that this play is especially relevant today for another reason. We are living at a time when the moral foundation of our society is suffering from a steady erosion, the equations between good and evil are becoming confused, human goodness is becoming a rarity.

Sankhapurer Sukanya (*The Good Person of Szechwan*) reminds us of the eternal tussle between good and evil and inspires us to think in terms of the well-being of both the individual and of the society at large.

Rudraprasad Sengupta

Sankhapurer Sukanya

Khadir Gondi

Sajano Bagan

The story of *Sajano Bagan* [The Orchard Bountiful] is an interesting one, but at its core stands this man who loves trees so passionately. In my *desh*, I've seen women gathering and crying around a big tree, a nut or a mango tree, cut down at the trunk—one of these trees had stood there for so long, close to the house—and lighting lamps at the stump in the evening! I know a man who'd say, 'Walking along the path, I'm never scared, for I know that the trees are walking along with me.' That's how people who belong to a land of waters and forests would feel. I knew closely an old man just like that.

Manoj Mitra

Naishabhoj

. . . *Shobhajatra* . . . had its limitations; the production, too, had its problems. But I was able to accomplish some new things. There was something about the writing too. I had gone on a shoot to Mahishadal in Medinipur. We were staying at the mansion of the Diwan, which was as grand as that of the zamindar. The Diwan's family was in a bad state at the time. The head of the family and his wife invited a few of us to lunch one day. We had seen him moving around, dhoti down to his knees, gun in hand. The place was in a shambles, the old edifice crumbling; the surviving walls covered with moss. At the centre of the courtyard lay an old abandoned *ratha* [a ceremonial chariot used once a year to carry the deities of Jagannatha, Balarama and Subhadra in procession]. While serving us, the lady of the house had a lot to tell us. She began haltingly—she sounded embarrassed and awkward—then continued in an undertone. 'We never have a chance to taste a mango from all those trees in our mango grove,' she said. 'They come from all over the village and even from beyond and pick them all.' 'Can't you stop them?' 'What can I tell them? They tell us, you've eaten enough of these, your ancestors too, who were horrible people, arch villains. Stop us if you dare!' She told us how they'd even take the doors and windows off the hinges—'We can't do a thing about it!' she said. 'With all the vicious tales in circulation about our forefathers, my father, my grandfather, up to fourteen generations back. Such a horrendous load of scandals! We just can't push the load out of our way, and take a stand with our heads held high.' There were just the two of them—husband and wife. Their children probably lived elsewhere. They left me with a strange feeling.

One can make theatre out of such an impression, or a memory of a place, or a sight that sticks, even without any training in theatre. One can draw lessons from such experiences. The more I thought of the scene in the daytime, in the long afternoons, in the night—we lived there all those days, through the days—I conjured up the *ratha* as it looked, covered by moss, in the morning; the daily chores that the couple went through; how they perceived their immediate surroundings; how they recalled the past, how the man brought his gun down . . . all those sights and images glowed so clear and bright in my memory that in my enactment I could just remain faithful to those impressions, and get the same experience out of my actors, and in the process I could get quite a few striking scenes in my production. I had succeeded in drawing the pictures faithfully from memory. That gave me a lot of joy. The play had a lot of pictures, impressions that proved to be quite effective. There was a song that I almost picturized. The elder sister sings a song while offering water to a thirsty Muslim peasant. The younger sister carries on from the *antara* [the part between the refrain and the final musical exposition in a song] in another scene. The same song stretches over two scenes, with the musical accompaniment bridging the break. There was a sense of satisfaction at the end of it all.

Manoj Mitra

Shobhajatra

Galpo Hekim Saheb

Parabas

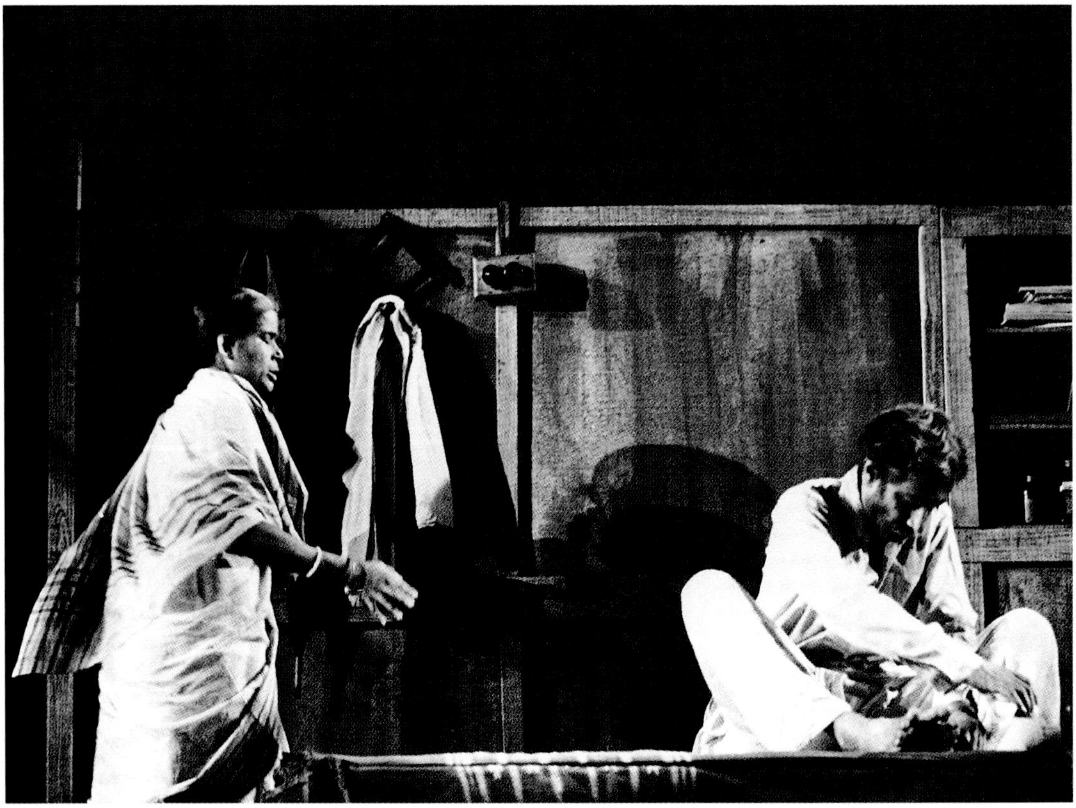

Bela Abelar Galpo

Neelam Neelam

Pratyasha

Uttaradhikar

Care Kori Na

. . . as I started working on *Care Kori Na* [We Don't Care!], I realized that a Grips production depends very much on how the playwright has conceived and structured the play. Grips is not just a theatrical construction of the children's whimsical world with a certain compassion and love for the little ones, but the result of an ideological comprehension of the children's situation in modern society . . . as I deal with my own situation in this society as a woman and mother, somewhere I [also] relate to / identify with the Grips plays because I feel the concerns are the same. The oppression of women that I have seen and felt in my own milieu, the urban middle-class milieu, has been more invisible than visible—benign, gentle, protective on the surface, but tough and hard underneath. The suppression of children has the same invisibility . . . Once I chose the option of relating to the similar oppression of children, I had the right balance of the objective and the subjective, knowing the child as a mother, and reading her /his oppression as a woman.

Jayoti Bose

Beda

Rudali

Rudali

For one and a half months I was very disturbed about the ending of the play [Rudali]. Mahaswetadi's story ends in idealism—the prostitutes become *rudalis*. I knew I had to keep that scene in the play, but I felt that this was not real, this was not how things happen in life. It was also suggested to me that the scene in which Sanichari gets the news of Bikhni's death should be the last sequence, but that didn't appeal to me. I tried to visualize the last sequence differently, with Sanichari standing alone, but still it was lacking something, it was not coming out well. The question was, 'Why did she go off with the group? Why is she standing there alone? What is she waiting for?' Then this present ending came to me.

I didn't want to treat this story in a sentimental way and make it a mere melodrama. Initially I thought that the last scene should be rustic and stylized, but this was not coming to me. It was not looking right. Eventually I realized that by stylizing the last sequence I could actually heighten the impact. Yet I managed to refrain from letting it get emotional. I like treating plays in an intelligent way, without letting them become emotional.

Usha Ganguli

Mushtijog

The greatest crisis faced by the group theatre movement today is, I feel, financial crisis. Instances of theatre groups going into dissolution are increasing every day and the situation will worsen as the days go by, as running a theatre group is becoming tough—the number of shows we have to put up, the finances involved in production and publicity, are escalating and it has become a sheer existential problem these days. Previously, too, the groups were not exactly well off, but then it wasn't so much a question of existence as it is today. Groups could do good theatre and exist. It wasn't necessary for their plays to be 'hits'.

Dwijen Banerjee

Meghnadbadh Kabya

Meghnadbadh Kabya

Meghnadbadh Kabya

Tiktiki

Fast expiring time
Comes to centre in a tiny dot,
The circle of light dwindles,
Gathering darkness around itself,
The darkness building up to a yearning
For the luminescence of a procession of scenes
Glowing out of the obscure magic of darkness.
One by one, plains and homesteads,
Forests and beaches
Glow into view,
With people in their midst
Tearing the darkness apart,
The glow in their eyes spreading far and wide,
When fast expiring time
Rivets in a tiny dot.

Soumitra Chatterjee.
7 January 1997

The difference between group theatre and commercial theatre is getting blurred. Group theatres were created on certain ideological precepts . . . if we go back to the sixties, we realize how with the breaking up of the IPTA, small groups were formed and how the old guard tried to cling on to the ideology of their times—maybe they failed, but they could usher in some change in the theatre scene in the sixties. Things have changed with time . . . the political atmosphere has also changed and with it several other factors which have a direct bearing on theatre. In the past, the group theatre movement in Calcutta used to consist of fifteen or twenty groups at the most and there would invariably be a scope for interaction among them. I'll give you an example. I was with the Little Theatre Group (LTG) in those days. We came to know that Shyamal Ghosh had produced an extraordinary play, *Brishti Brishti*. A large number of us from LTG went to see the play and we also spread the word around. This was possible in those days; but now with three hundred groups it just isn't feasible. I feel that the passion for theatre is missing these days and with it some basic tenets like discipline—something that was almost congenital to the groups in the sixties.

Runu Chowdhury

Aajker Ha Ja Ba Ra La

Gantabya

I can do adaptations of foreign plays all my life if I feel that's the need of our times. If I do Indian plays, I'll work only with contemporary playwrights—as far as I am concerned, it doesn't matter whether the play is an original or an adaptation. I always look for certain elements in it; for example, I'll look for how the play deals with the contradictions in modern society and whether it has been able to reach the psyche of the reader/audience . . . it is extremely important for me to say something relevant to the present context through my kind of theatre. I don't bother about whether my play is realistic or naturalistic, Indian or foreign—the statement is important, the form is not.

Suman Mukhopadhyay

Suman Mukhopadhyay : What we really need to think about is, had the Left leadership not come into power in West Bengal, what difference would it have made?

Jayoti Bose : I don't think that any questioning or introspection really happened either in the case of politics or in the case of theatre. In the post-IPTA phase, all political plays had one theme—oppression. The context changed every time. Sometimes it was the oppression of the peasant, sometimes the labourer, but these plays did not really take up anything more varied. This trend has emerged again and again. A proper introspection, at least in the case of theatre, has been absent.

Harimadhab Mukhopadhyay: Before the Left Front came to power we thought we were moving towards a definite ideological stand (even if we shelved direct ideology and direct politics) which would herald some kind of a change—a social change, a progressive change—and our work in theatre continued in this way. This was before the Front took over. When the desired change in politics came through, with the Front coming to power, the relationships started changing and dilution set in. As usual, we could not comprehend the extent of this dilution.

Janmadin

Kamalkamini

When I was a child, my mother would tell me, 'You have a remarkable memory.' Later, my eldest sister, too, would pay me the same compliment. I had once recounted an old incident to my sister. She asked me, 'Do you remember it all?' I said, 'Yes.' She was surprised, 'But how can you? You were barely four years old, then.'

When I acted *Kamalkamini*, a one woman piece, I relived my own memories. When I sang 'Come, oh Come, oh daughter of the Earth . . .' I remembered the scene in *Seeta*, with Prafullabala singing it offstage. I had acted the child Atreyee, my mother Prova Devi playing Seeta, the daughter of the Earth, and the legendary Sisirkumar Bhaduri, my uncle, Rama, way back in the 1940s.

I did my first role in *Maya*, as a dead boy carried on to the stage. At the end of the third performance, my mother went up to Sisirkumar—she called him Baba [i.e. father], don't ask me why. She would also call him guru, raise her hands to her head whenever she referred to him. She went up to Sisirkumar, and told him, 'Baba, can't you leave Chhoto [i.e. the little one]—that's what I was called—out of this? I can't bear the sight of it.' It hit Sisirkumar like a shock. For he recalled the incident in Rangpur. My elder sister Sagarika had started acting at the age of six. Those were the days of touring theatre. There were more performances on tour than stage performances in the city, the tours running to fifteen days, twenty days, twenty-five days, to two months at a stretch. The companies travelled long distances, often to present-day Bangladesh, to Dhaka, to Chattagram, to Faridpur, to Rangpur. On one of these tours, my elder sister died of diphtheria in Rangpur, after running a fever for two days. *Seeta* was scheduled for that evening. It was my mother who told me, that evening the whole of Rangpur had come out to the cremation ground, where Sisirkumar announced the cancellation of the evening's performance, and told the crowd that their tickets would be valid for the following evening's performance. But mother intervened. She said, 'No, you can't disappoint them. They have come from long distances. It's not fair to send them back today, and ask them to come tomorrow. Can you bring my dead child back to me? Will she return? Let the show be held. The show must carry on.' The play was staged that evening. But ever since—maybe from that memory itself—mother had a very special affection for me. She loved me immensely. She told Sisirkumar, 'Can't you drop that scene?' Sisirkumar could sense the hurt, and said, 'Yes, I'd drop it.'

In *Kamalkamini*, the ageing actress I enact talks of her son dying of cholera, and her performance that night as Marjina, the dancing slave girl, in the play *Ali Baba*—a takeoff on the death of my own sister and my mother's performance!

Ketaki Dutta

Baghu Manna

Daradi

One of Rangakarmee's earliest productions was Brecht's dramatization of Gorky's *Mother*. Rangakarmee returned to Bertolt Brecht for his centenary, with *Mother Courage*, not so much as a centenary tribute or an experiment, but more as a response to the spate of violence all over the world in the name of religion, and as an endeavour to draw people's attention to the central concern of all times, and ours in particular—the survival of humanity. *Mother Courage* is not a tragedy: it is an avowal of humanity.

The production treats the text as a classic, and prefers to break it down to its bare essentials. The cart of *Mother Courage*, one of modern theatre's most cherished icons, holds centre stage, but there is little attempt to follow the rules and codes supposed to be characteristic of a Brechtian 'style'. The only Brechtian principle that comes into view is the tearing down of the illusion of theatre, turning theatre inside out, so that it acquires a more direct charge.

Usha Ganguli

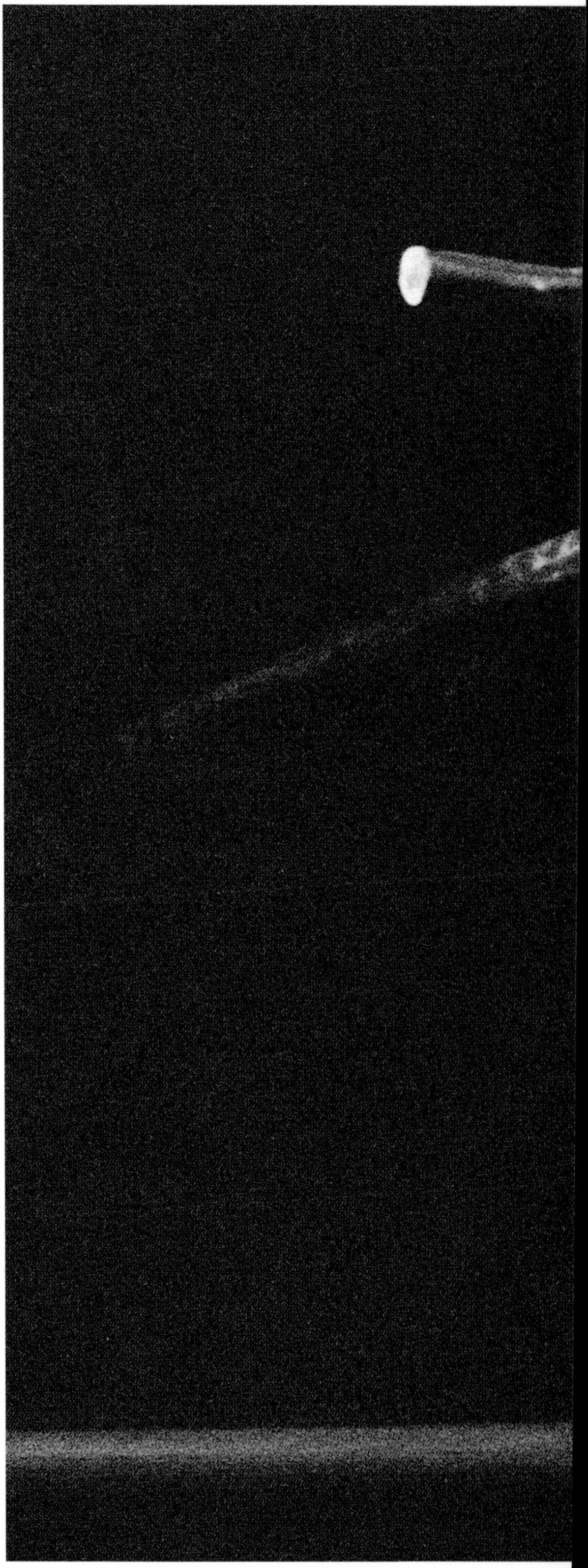

Himmat Mai

Theatrography

Page 5-11. *Char Adhyay*. NOVEL. Rabindranath Tagore. ADPT. and DIR. Sombhu Mitra. PROD. Bohurupee. PREM. Srirangam, 21 August 1951.

Page 13-17. *Putulkhela*. PLAY. Henrik Ibsen's *A Doll's House*. ADPT. and DIR. Sombhu Mitra. PROD. Bohurupee. PREM. Mahajati Sadan, 10 January 1958.

Page 18-19. *Dashachakra*. PLAY. Henrik Ibsen's *An Enemy of the People*. ADPT. Shanti Basu. DIR. Sombhu Mitra. PROD. Bohurupee. PREM. Srirangam, 1 June 1952 [revived 28 October 1962].

Page 20-21. *Tughlaq*. PLAY. Girish Karnad. TRNS. Chittaranjan Ghosh. DIR. Shyamanand Jalan. PROD. Bangla Natmancha Pratistha Samiti. PREM. Kalamandir, 4 December 1972.

Page 23. *Mudrarakshasa*. PLAY. Vishakhadatta. ADPT. Ajitesh Bandyopadhyay from Jyotirindranath Tagore's Bengali translation. DIR. Ajitesh Bandyopadhyay. PROD. Bangla Natmancha Pratistha Samiti. PREM. Kalamandir, 7 June 1970.

Page 24-25. *Galileor Jiban*. PLAY. Bertolt Brecht's *The Life of Galileo*. ADPT. Mohit Chattopadhyay. DIR. Fritz Bennewitz. PROD. Calcutta Repertory Theatre (CRT). PREM. Academy of Fine Arts, 25 December 1980.

Page 26. *Pagla Ghora*. PLAY. Badal Sircar. DIR. Sombhu Mitra. PROD. Bohurupee. PREM. Academy of Fine Arts, 28 February 1971.

Page 27. *Chop! Adalat Cholchhey*. PLAY. Vijay Tendulkar. TRNS. S.B. Joshi and Nitish Sen. DIR. Sombhu Mitra. PROD. Bohurupee. PREM. Kalamandir, 9 December 1971.

Page 28-30. *Raja*. PLAY. Rabindranath Tagore. DIR. Sombhu Mitra. PROD. Bohurupee. PREM. New Empire, 13 June 1964.

Page 34-35. *Dakghar*. PLAY. Rabindranath Tagore. DIR. Tripti Mitra. PROD. Bohurupee. PREM. New Empire, 24 February 1957 [revived 26 July 1973].

Page 36-37. *Aparajita*. PLAY. Nitish Sen. DIR. Tripti Mitra. PROD. Bohurupee. PREM. Kalamandir basement, 7 September 1971.

Page 38-39. *Sutarang*. PLAY. John Steinbeck's *Of Mice and Men*. ADPT. and DIR. Tripti Mitra. PROD. Bohurupee. PREM. Academy of Fine Arts, 25 December 1975.

Page 40. *Pterodactyl*. PLAY. Indra Upadhyay. DIR. Tripti Mitra. PROD. Bohurupee. PREM. Academy of Fine Arts, 10 October 1972.

Page 41. *Hajar Churashir Ma*. NOVEL. Mahasweta Devi. ADPT. and DIR. Tripti Mitra. PROD. Arabdha Natya Vidhyalay. PREM. 1984.

Page 42. *Raktakarabi*. PLAY. Rabindranath Tagore. DIR. Tripti Mitra. PROD. Arabdha Natya Vidhyalay. PREM. Academy of Fine Arts, 1 January 1984.

Page 50-51. *Buro Shaliker Ghadey Ron*. PLAY. Michael Madhusudan Dutt. DIR. Utpal Dutt. PROD. Little Theatre Group. PREM. Marcus Square, Calcutta, at Banga Sanskriti Sammelan, 1955.

Page 52-53. *Manusher Adhikarey*. PLAY. and DIR. Utpal Dutt. PROD. LTG. PREM. Minerva, 14 July 1968.

Page 54-55. *Leniner Dak*. PLAY. and DIR. Utpal Dutt. PROD. LTG. PREM. Minerva, 16 November 1969.

Page 58-59. *Tiner Talwar*. PLAY. and DIR. Utpal Dutt. PROD. People's Little

Theatre. PREM. Rabindra Sadan, 12 August 1971.

Page 60. *Barricade.* PLAY. and DIR. Utpal Dutt. PROD. PLT. PREM. Kalamandir, 25 December 1972.

Page 63. *Danrao Pathikbar.* PLAY. and DIR. Utpal Dutt. PROD. PLT. PREM. Calcutta University Institute Hall, 4 December 1980.

Page 64-65. *Duswapner Nagari.* PLAY. and DIR. Utpal Dutt. PROD. PLT. PREM. Kalamandir, 16 May 1974.

Page 66. *Chaitali Rater Swapna.* PLAY. William Shakespeare's *A Midsummer Night's Dream.* ADPT. and DIR. Utpal Dutt. PROD. Natya Akademi. PREM. Rabindra Sadan, 15 January 1989.

Page 68. *Titumir.* PLAY. AND DIR. Utpal Dutt. PROD. PLT. PREM. Rabindra Sadan, 26 January 1978.

Page 74-75. *Tin Paisar Pala.* PLAY. Bertolt Brecht's *The Threepenny Opera.* ADPT. and DIR. Ajitesh Bandyopadhyay. PROD. Nandikar. PREM. New Empire, 14 December 1969.

Page 76. *Bhalo Manush.* PLAY. Bertolt Brecht's *The Good Person of Szechwan.* ADPT. and DIR. Ajitesh Bandyopadhyay. PROD. Nandikar. PREM. 15 February 1974.

Page 77-79. *Antigone.* PLAY. Sophocles's *Antigone.* ADPT. Chittaranjan Ghosh. DIR. Rudraprasad Sengupta. PROD. Nandikar. PREM. Academy of Fine Arts, 25 March 1975.

Page 80. *Nati Binodini.* PLAY. Chittaranjan Ghosh. DIR. Ajitesh Bandyopadhyay. PROD. Nandikar. PREM. Kalamandir, 6 December 1972.

Page 81. *Bitangsha.* PLAY. Joseph Kesselring's *Arsenic and Old Lace.* ADPT. and DIR. Ajitesh Bandyopadhyay. PROD. Nandikar. PREM. Rangana, 27 December 1971.

Page 82-87. *Paap Punya.* PLAY. Leo Tolstoy's *The Power of Darkness.* ADPT. and DIR. Ajitesh Bandyopadhyay. PROD. Nandimukh. PREM. Sisir Mancha, 28 August 1978.

Page 100. *Ballabhpurer Rupkatha.* PLAY. AND DIR. Badal Sircar. PROD. Satabdi. PREM. Academy of Fine Arts, 28 November 1970.

Page 102-103. *Androcles O Singha.* PLAY. Bernard Shaw's *Androcles and the Lion.* ADPT. and DIR. Badal Sircar. PROD. Satabdi. PREM. Sindhu Bhavan, 29 July 1991.

Page 104-105. *Hattamalar Oparey.* PLAY. and DIR. Badal Sircar. PROD. Satabdi. PREM. Theosophical Society Hall, 22 July 1977.

Page 106. *Banglar Mati.* PLAY. Tulsi Lahiri. DIR. Sabitabrata Datta. PROD. Anandam. PREM. Mohammad Ali Park, 9 March 1956.

Page 108-109. *Kolkatar Hamlet.* PLAY. AND DIR. Asit Bose. PROD. Calcutta People's Arts Theatre. PREM. Kalamandir, 16 August 1973.

Page 110. *Bidehi.* PLAY. Henrik Ibsen's *Ghosts.* TRNS. and DIR. Soumitra Chattopadhyay. PROD. Abhinetri Sangha. PREM. Rabindra Sadan, 7 December 1973.

Page 111. *Dansagar.* STORY. Munshi Premchand's *Kafan.* ADPT. Debashis Majumdar. DIR. Nilkantha Sengupta. PROD. Theatre Commune. PREM. Rabindra Sadan, 22 August 1976.

Page 112-113. *Pontu Laha.* PLAY. Bertolt Brecht's *Puntila and His Man Matti.* ADPT. and DIR. Sekhar Chatterjee. PROD. Theatre Unit. PREM. 24 February 1975.

Page 115. *Chhayanot.* PLAY. Utpal Dutt. DIR. Robi Ghosh. PROD. Chalachal. PREM. 1976.

Page 116. *Jagannath.* STORY. Lu Xun's *The True Story of Ah Q.* ADPT. and DIR. Arun Mukherjee. PROD. Chetana. PREM. Academy of Fine Arts, 8 February 1977.

Page 118-119. *Antigone.* PLAY. Sophocles's *Antigone.* ADPT. Alokeranjan Dasgupta. DIR. Hansguenther Heyme. PROD. Max Mueller Bhavan. PREM. St. Paul's Cathedral grounds, 6 April 1979.

Page 120. *Rajrakta.* PLAY. Mohit Chattopadhyay. DIR. Bibhash Chakraborty. PROD. Theatre Workshop. PREM. Rangana, 25 January 1971.

Page 122-123. *Chakbhanga Madhu.* PLAY. Manoj Mitra. DIR. Bibhash Chakraborty. PROD. Theatre Workshop. PREM. Rangana, 16 May 1972.

Page 124-125. *Narak Guljar.* PLAY. Manoj Mitra. DIR. Bibhash Chakraborty. PROD. Theatre Workshop. PREM. Academy of Fine Arts, 27 December 1976.

Page 126-127. *Schweik Gelo Juddhey.* PLAY. Bertolt Brecht's *Schweik in the Second World War.* ADPT. Ashok Mukhopadhyay. DIR. Bibhash Chakraborty. PROD. Theatre Workshop. PREM. Academy of Fine Arts, 1 September 1981.

Page 128-129. *Madhab Malanchi Kainya.* ADPT. Bibhash Chakraborty [from a ballad in the Myemensingh Geetika]. DIR. Bibhash Chakraborty. PROD. Anya Theatre. PREM. Sisir Mancha, 17 February 1988.

Page 132. *Mrichhakatik.* PLAY. Sudraka's *Mrichhakatikam.* ADPT. Kumar Roy [from the Bengali trnsl. by Jyotirindranath Tagore]. DIR. Kumar Roy. PROD. Bohurupee. PREM. Academy of Fine Arts, 9 September 1979.

Page 134-135. *Galileo.* PLAY. Bertolt Brecht's *The Life of Galileo.* ADPT. and DIR. Kumar Roy. PROD. Bohurupee. PREM. Academy of Fine Arts, 12 October 1980.

Page 136. *Nindapankey.* PLAY. Jean Paul Sartre's *Crime Passionel.* TRNS. Arun Mitra. DIR. Kumar Roy. PROD. Bohurupee. PREM. Academy of Fine Arts, 1 December 1990.

Page 137. *Akbar Birbal.* PLAY. Sisirkumar Das. DIR. Kumar Roy. PROD. Bohurupee. PREM. Academy of Fine Arts, 1 May 1993.

Page 139. *Rajdarshan.* PLAY. Manoj Mitra. DIR. Kumar Roy. PROD. Bohurupee. PREM. Academy of Fine Arts, 21 February 1982.

Page 140-142. *Sankhapurer Sukanya.* PLAY. Bertolt Brecht's *The Good Person of Szechwan.* ADPT. and DIR. Rudraprasad Sengupta. PROD. Nandikar. PREM. Academy of Fine Arts, 23 August 1990.

Page 143. *Khadir Gondi.* PLAY. Bertolt Brecht's *The Caucasian Chalk Circle.* ADPT. and DIR. Rudraprasad Sengupta. PROD. Nandikar. PREM. Academy of Fine Arts, 30 March 1978.

Page 144. *Sajano Bagan.* PLAY. AND DIR. Manoj Mitra. PROD. Sundaram. PREM. Muktangan, 7 November 1977.

Page 145. *Naishabhoj.* PLAY. AND DIR. Manoj Mitra. PROD. Sundaram. PREM. Rabindra Sadan, 8 January 1986.

Page 148. *Shobhajatra.* PLAY. AND DIR. Manoj Mitra. PROD. Sundaram. PREM. Academy of Fine Arts, 8 September 1991.

Page 149. *Galpo Hekim Saheb.* PLAY. AND DIR. Manoj Mitra. PROD. Sundaram. PREM. Academy of Fine Arts, 28 March 1994.

Page 150-151. *Parabas.* PLAY. AND DIR. Manoj Mitra. PROD. Sundaram. PREM. Academy of Fine Arts, 9 September 1975.

Page 152. *Bela Abelar Galpo.* PLAY. Arnold Wesker's *Chicken Soup with Barley.* ADPT. and DIR. Ashok Mukhopadhyay. PROD. Theatre Workshop.

PREM. Academy of Fine Arts, 13 June 1986.

Page 153. *Neelam Neelam.* PLAY. Arthur Miller's *The Price.* ADPT. and DIR. Asit Mukhopadhyay. PROD. Gandhar. PREM. Academy of Fine Arts, 3 June 1987.

Page 154. *Pratyasha.* PLAY. Chandra Dastidar. DIR. Jochhan Dastidar. PROD. Charbak. PREM. Academy of Fine Arts, 1 January 1989.

Page 155. *Uttaradhikar.* PLAY. Mahesh Elkunchwar's *Wada Chirebandi.* ADPT. Subrata Nandy. DIR. Sohag Sen. PROD. Ensemble. PREM. Gyan Manch, 24 February 1989.

Page 156-157. *Care Kori Na!!* PLAY. Volker Ludwig's *Max and Milli.* ADPT. and DIR. Jayoti Bose. PROD. Sutrapat. PREM. Max Mueller Bhavan, 27 February 1993.

Page 158. *Beda.* PLAY. Lansford Wilson's *Fences.* ADPT. and DIR. Ashok Mukhopadhyay. PROD. Theatre Workshop. PREM. 22 March 1991.

Page 159-161. *Rudali.* STORY. Mahesweta Devi. ADPT. Usha Ganguli with Samar Chatterjee, Partha Banerjee, Subir Mukherjee. DIR. Usha Ganguli. PROD. Rangakarmee. PREM. Gyan Manch, 28 December 1992.

Page 162-163. *Mushtijog.* PLAY. Arun Mukherjee. DIR. Dwijen Banerjee. PROD. Sangstab. PREM. Sisir Mancha, 22 April 1993.

Page 164-167. *Meghnadbadh Kabya.* POEM. Michael Madhusudan Dutt. ADPT. and DIR. Gautam Haldar. PROD. Nandikar. PREM. Academy of Fine Arts, 11 May 1995.

Page 168. *Tiktiki.* PLAY. Peter Shaffer's *Sleuth.* ADPT. and DIR. Soumitra Chattopadhyay. PROD. Swapnasandhanee. PREM. Academy of Fine Arts, 29 May 1995.

Page 171. *Ajker Ha Ja Ba Ra La.* PLAY. Partha Chattopadhyay. DIR. Runu Chowdhury. PROD. Kushilab. PREM. Academy of Fine Arts, 30 June 1995.

Page 172. *Gantabya.* PLAY. AND DIR. Suman Mukhopadhyay. PROD. Chetana. PREM. Academy of Fine Arts, 10 February 1997.

Page 175. *Janmadin.* PLAY. William Gibson's *The Miracle Worker.* ADPT. Mohit Chattopadhyay. DIR. Asit Mukhopadhyay. PROD. Chupkatha. PREM. G. D. Birla Sabhaghar, 19 August 1997.

Page 176-177. *Kamalkamini.* PLAY. and DIR. Ishita Mukhopadhyay. PROD. Ushnik. PREM. Sisir Mancha, 5 November 1993.

Page 180. *Baghu Manna.* STORY. Sirshendu Mukhopadhyay. ADPT. Arun Mukherjee. DIR. Biplabketan Chakravarty. PROD. Theatrewallah. PREM. Academy of Fine Arts, 16 July 1996.

Page 181. *Daradi.* PLAY. Arunshankar Moitra. DIR. Chandan Sen. PROD. Natya Anan, PREM. Sisir Mancha, 13 August 1998.

Page 182-183. *Himmat Mai.* PLAY. Bertolt Brecht's *Mother Courage and Her Children.* ADPT. and DIR. Usha Ganguli. PROD. Rangakarmee. PREM. Academy of Fine Arts, 15 August 1998.

[All these plays were premiered in Calcutta, unless mentioned otherwise. Though the dates of the premieres have been maintained for historical reasons, all photographs in this volume are post-1966.]

Sources and References

[All texts and translations by Samik Bandyopadhyay unless mentioned otherwise.]

Page 1. On Sombhu Mitra by Samik Bandyopadhyay.

Page 11. Sombhu Mitra on *Char Adhyay*, from the *TDR* special issue on Asian Theatre, 1971-72.

Page 12. Khaled Chowdhury on the stage design of *Putulkhela*, from an article in *Parichay*, volume 35, number 6, B.S. 1372 [January 1966]

Page 18. Sombhu Mitra on his production of *Dashachakra* from *The Doyen of Indian Theatre*, documentary on Sombhu Mitra, directed and produced by Raja Sen, 1998.

Page 21. Extract from the paper presented by Ajitesh Bandyopadhyay at the Natyasashtra Seminar organized by Anamika, 7-11 March 1980. Translated from the Bengali by S. B.

Page 29. Tripti Mitra in Kapila Vatsyayan, ed. *Concepts of Space: Ancient and Modern*, New Delhi: Indira Gandhi National Centre for the Arts (IGNCA) and Abhinav Publications, 1991.

Page 31. On Tripti Mitra by S. B.

Page 37. Tripti Mitra in Kapila Vatsyayan, ed. *Concepts of Space: Ancient and Modern*, New Delhi: Indira Gandhi National Centre for the Arts (IGNCA) and Abhinav Publications, 1991.

Page 43. On Utpal Dutt by S. B.

Page 51. Utpal Dutt, *Towards a Revolutionary Theatre*, Calcutta: M C Sarkar, 1995, pp. 14-15.

Page 53. Ibid. pp. 15-16.

Page 54. Utpal Dutt interviewed by S.B. in *Enact*, nos. 68-69, August-September 1972.

Page 55. Excerpt from the commentary for the five-part television serial *In Search of Theatre*, written, directed and produced by Utpal Dutt for Doordarshan, 1986.

Page 56. Utpal Dutt, *Towards a Revolutionary Theatre*, Calcutta: M C Sarkar, 1995, p. 62.

Page 60. Ibid. pp. 93-94.

Page 65. Translated by S.B. from the original Bengali poem 'Duswapner Nagari' by Utpal Dutt.

Page 67. Excerpted from the director's note in the Natya Akademi brochure for the play.

Page 69. On Ajitesh Bandyopadhyay by S. B.

Page 74. Keya Chakravarty interviewed by Santiranjan Chatterjee in *Amrita*, 25 December 1975. Translation S.B.

Page 78. Alokeranjan Dasgupta's poem in Bengali translated by S. B.

Page 88. Seventies to Nineties: Overview by S. B.

Page 100. Excerpt from Badal Sircar's presentation *Voyages in the Theatre*, Shri Ram Memorial Lectures IV, New Delhi: Shri Ram Centre for Performing Arts.

Page 105. Excerpted from Badal Sircar's poem 'The Night is Green' in Anjali Basu ed. *Nana Mukh*, Calcutta, November 1988.

Page 106. Sabitabrata Datta interviewed by Natya Shodh Sansthan, 23

February 1984. Translation S. B.

Page 109. Excerpt from interview with Asit Bose for the Seagull Theatre Quarterly, 1998. Translation S. B.

Page 112. Sekhar Chatterjee introducing his production of *Pontu Laha/ Puntila* at the International Seminar on Brecht at Hong Kong, 1981, quoted by S.B. in 'Brecht in Bengali/ West Bengal', *Rangavarta*, no. 55, Calcutta, November 1994.

Page 116. Arun Mukherjee interviewed for *STQ*, 1998. Translation S. B.

Page 121. Bibhash Chakraborty interviewed for *STQ*, 1998. Translation S. B

Page 123. Manoj Mitra interviewed for *STQ*, 1998. Translation S. B.

Page 126. Translated by S.B. from 'Amar Chokhey Chaplin-er Abhinayreeti' [The Way I Look at Chaplin's Acting Style], in Bishwa Roy, ed. *Bibhash: Byaktigata O Shilpagata* [Bibhash: Personal and Artistic], Calcutta: Pustak Bipani, 1999.

Page 129. Director's note in the *Madhab Malanchi Kainya* brochure.

Page 131, 133, 136, 137, 138. Kumar Roy interviewed for *STQ*, 1999. Translation Sudeshna Banerjee.

Page 141. Excerpt from the director's note in the *Sankapurer Sukanya* brochure.

Page 144, 146. Manoj Mitra interviewed for *STQ*, 1998. Translation S. B.

Page 157. Jayoti Bose interviewed in *STQ*, no. 3, October 1994.

Page 161. Usha Ganguli interviewed in *STQ*, no.1, January 1994.

Page 163. Dwijen Banerjee interviewed for *STQ*, 1998. Translation Sudeshna Banerjee.

Page 169. Scribbled in the promptbook as he waited in the wings for a stage entry in the play *Tiktiki* (*Sleuth*), a crime play, a black comedy set in a battleground of classes. Translation S. B.

Page 170. Runu Chowdhury interviewed for *STQ*, 1998. Translation Sudeshna Banerjee.

Page 173. Suman Mukhopadhyay interviewed for *STQ*, 1998. Translation Sudeshna Banerjee.

Page 174. Excerpt from the discussion in the Round Table on Bengali Theatre organized by The Seagull Foundation for the Arts, 9-10 July 1998.

Page 178. Ketaki Dutta interviewed for *STQ*, 1994. Translation S.B.

Page 182. Director's note in the *Himmat Mai* brochure.

Contributors

AJITESH BANDYOPADHYAY (1933-83), actor-director in theatre and cinema, playwright and translator. Led the theatre group Nandikar from 1960 to the late seventies.

ALOKERANJAN DASGUPTA (b. 1933), poet and critic, settled in Germany as Professor at Heidelberg University.

ARUN MUKHERJEE (b. 1937), playwright, actor, director, has led the theatre group Chetana from 1972.

ASIT BOSE (b. 1943), actor, director, playwright, began theatre career in LTG/PLT under Utpal Dutt, breaking away to form CPAT; career in jatra for over a decade; has directed/co-directed documentaries on Jyotsna Dutta, Ustad Abdul Karim Khan and Ustad Faiyaz Khan.

BADAL SIRCAR (b. 1925), professionally engineer and town-planner; author of *Ebong Indrajit*, landmark modern Indian play; ideologue and director of a free theatre movement spearheaded by his own theatre group, Satabdi.

BIBHASH CHAKRABORTY (b. 1937), actor–director, began theatre career as actor with Nandikar, breaking off in 1966 to form Theatre Workshop which he led till 1985, when he formed Anya Theatre. Was employed in Doordarshan, 1974-89. Has directed plays for several groups and television serials.

DWIJEN BANERJEE (b. 1949), actor, director, started theatre career in 1974 with Subrata Nandy's Theatre Front, moving on to Neelkantha Sengupta's Theatre Commune, before forming his group Sangstab in 1983, which he leads.

HARIMADHAB MUKHOPADHYAY (b. 1941), playwright, director, actor, pioneered theatre movement in Balurghat, South Dinajpur with his group Triteertha, which he has led since 1969.

JAYOTI BOSE (b. 1953), actress, began career in Theatre Workshop, acted with Sundaram and Ensemble before starting theatre group, Sutrapat, which has been associated with the Grips Theatre movement in West Bengal.

KETAKI DUTTA (b. 1934), singer-actress, daughter of the legendary Prova Devi, began her career with Sisirkumar Bhaduri at Srirangam, was a leading actress in the commercial theatres Minerva and Rangmahal, before producing and playing the female lead in the popular *Antony Kabiyal* and *Baarbodhu*.

KEYA CHAKRABARTY (1942-77), actress, leading lady in several Nandikar productions.

KHALED CHOWDHURY (b.1919), stage designer, music director, folklorist and book designer.

KUMAR ROY (b. 1926), actor, director, playwright and designer, associated with Bohurupee for over fifty years, now leading the group.

MANOJ MITRA (b. 1938), playwright, director, stage and film actor. Has led the theatre group Sundaram from 1977.

RUDRAPRASAD SENGUPTA (b. 1935), actor, director, began his theatre career as actor in Nandikar, eventually coming to lead the group.

RUNU CHOWDHURY (b. 1943), actor, director, has led the theatre group

Kushilab since its inception in 1989.

SABITABRATA DATTA (b. 1924-95), singer, actor, collector of nationalist songs from the freedom movement, led theatre group Rupakar (1955-81), after a brief stint in Bohurupee. Acclaimed for his roles in *Byapika Biday*, *Chalachittachanchari*, *Lalan Fakir*, *Antony Kabiyal* in theatre, and in the film *Charankabi Mukundadas* (1968).

SAMIK BANDYOPADHYAY (b. 1940), editor, scholar, critic, writer, who has specialized in the arts, especially the performing arts and cinema; he has published widely in both Bengali and English.

SEKHAR CHATTERJEE (1924-90), actor, director, playwright, translator, led theatre groups Theatre Unit and Unity Theatre; best known for his productions of Brecht in Bengali, staged at the International Brecht Dialogue, Hong Kong.

SOMBHU MITRA (1915-97), actor, director, playwright, led the theatre group Bohurupee till the early seventies.

SOUMITRA CHATTOPADHYAY (b. 1935), poet, actor, director, came into prominence as hero of Ray's *Apur Sansar*, growing to become one of the foremost stars of the Bengali cinema and adapting, directing, writing plays for both the commercial and experimental theatres.

SUMAN MUKHOPADHYAY (b. 1966), actor, director, began career with Chetana, rising to prominence with his productions of *Coriolanus*, *Dain* and *Gantabya*.

TRIPTI MITRA (1925-93), actress, began career as leading lady in *Nabanna* (1944), played lead roles in Bohurupee plays till the late seventies; formed Arabdha as theatre school and group, writing and directing plays for it.

USHA GANGULI (b. 1945), trained as a Bharatnatyam dancer, acted with several Hindi groups before forming Rangakarmee which she now leads as actress-director.

UTPAL DUTT (1929-93), actor-director, playwright, ideologue; led the theatre groups Little Theatre Group and the People's Little Theatre. Was a major star in cinema, appearing in films by Ray, Sen, Ghatak and Ivory.

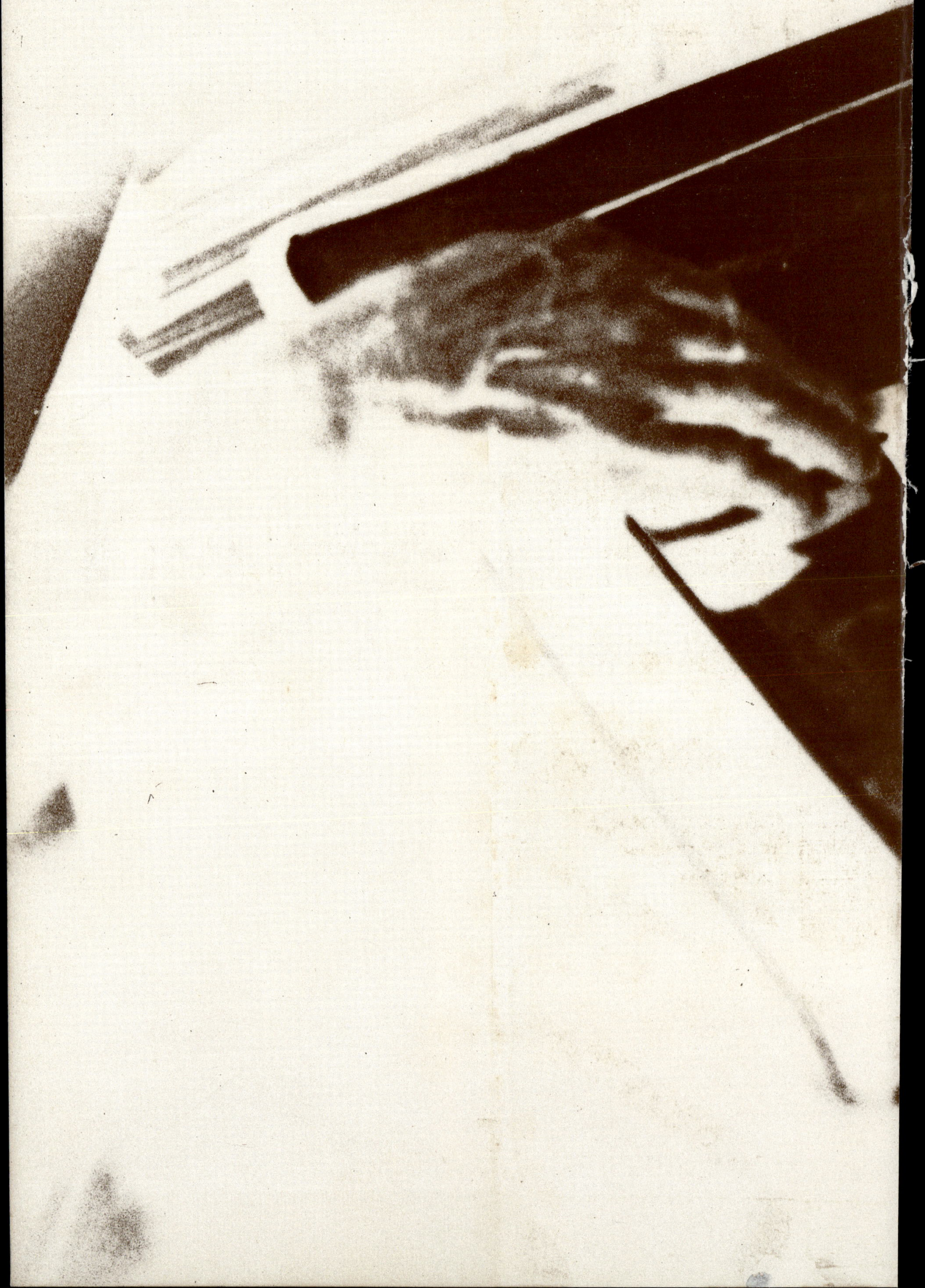